Mates, Dates

The Secret Story

Dates and *Truth, Dare* books, as well as the highly acclaimed *Cinnamon Girl* series. She lives in North London with her husband and cats.

Cathy spends most of her time locked in a shed at the bottom of the garden pretending to write books, but she is actually in there listening to music, hippie dancing and talking to her friends on email.

Apart from that, Cathy has joined the gym and spends more time than is good for her making up excuses as to why she hasn't got time to go.

Find out more about Cathy and her books at
www.cathyhopkins.com

Cathy Hopkins

Mates, Dates

The Secret Story

PICCADILLY PRESS • LONDON

Thanks to Brenda Gardner, Anne Clark and the fab team
at Piccadilly and to all those readers who wrote to me and said,
'We want more of Lucy and Tony from the Mates, Dates series.'
They inspired this book, so this is also dedicated to them.

First published in Great Britain in 2009
by Piccadilly Press Ltd,
5 Castle Road, London NW1 8PR

A catalogue record for this book is available from
the British Library.

ISBN: 978 1 84812 018 1

3 5 7 9 10 8 6 4 2

Cover design by Simon Davis

Printed in ░░░░░░░░░░░░░░░░░░ 0 4TD

Lucy

It was a moment that was to change my life for ever.

I was sitting in the passenger seat, staring out of the window as Dad drove us home. It was raining – which seemed fitting for the grey mood I was in.

'How was school?' asked Dad.

I shrugged my shoulders. 'OK,' I replied. I didn't feel like talking. I was thinking about Izzie. She's been my best mate since junior school but something weird has been going on lately. A new girl arrived at the end of the summer term. Nesta Williams. She created quite a stir. She's stunning for one thing – tall, dark-skinned with black hair like silk down her back, and she's so confident. She's everything I'm not. I'm small, blonde and totally unsure of who I am or where I fit in.

This September, we went into Year Nine and Izzie started hanging out with Nesta and now she's always like, Nesta said this, Nesta did that. I'm scared that Izzie feels that she's outgrown me, like I'm boring compared to her glam new mate. Or too childish.

The other night, we tried to get into a fifteen movie and we were turned away. I knew it was my fault because Izzie and Nesta both look sixteen. I couldn't kid myself otherwise thanks to Josie – a mean girl from our school who was there in the queue. She looked my way then called out for everyone to hear, 'Anyone can see the midget's underage,' and when she swanned into the movie with a bunch of Year Elevens, she said, 'Leave the children to play.' That hurt. And Nesta looked cross – probably because we hadn't got in and it was because of me. I think she felt embarrassed to be seen with me too. So . . . I'm not sure if there's going to be room for me in Izzie's life any more. She clearly wants to move on and hang with the more grown up cool crowd.

Dad slowed down the car as the traffic lights changed and it was then that I saw him. A vision of boy babeness. He was coming out of the school gates at St Michael's and he crossed the road in front of us. Dark. Handsome. Chiselled jaw. A Disney prince in a schoolboy's black-and-white uniform, alive and walking the streets of North London. My heart sped up. It really did – *boom banga bang* in my chest – and I felt my stomach twist as I watched him. He didn't see me. He was talking to another boy. They were laughing about something.

Ohmigod, I thought. *After all these months of looking for a boy and only finding weedy wombats. There he is.*

'Lucy, you're blushing,' said Izzie later that same day.

'No, I'm not,' I objected, although I felt colour flush to my cheeks. Izzie is lucky, she never blushes. She has the looks of a typical Irish colleen: dark hair, green eyes, pale skin. Pale skin that always looks cool and in control.

I hate that I blush, I thought. *It always gives my secrets away. I bet Nesta never blushes.* I've tried wearing pale make-up to hide my red cheeks but it doesn't work – nothing does and my embarrassment is always evident to anyone who happens to be looking at me.

Izzie raised an eyebrow and gave me a look as if to say, 'Pull the other one'. I turned away from her and the computer where we'd been checking our horoscopes. I'd gone straight round to her house as soon as I'd had supper.

'So. What's going on?' asked Izzie.

There was no point in hiding it. I could never keep anything from her for long and I was bursting to tell her my news. 'I'm in love,' I blurted.

'Brilliant,' said Izzie. 'Who's the lucky boy?'

I shrugged my shoulders. 'Don't know.'

'What do you mean, you don't know?'

'I haven't actually spoken to him yet.'

'Ah. Do you know his name?'

I shook my head. 'I know what school he goes to. St Michael's.'

Izzie smiled. 'I suppose that's a start. And, er . . . how do you know it's love?'

'I just do,' I replied. I did.

'OK,' said Izzie. 'You just do.'

I nodded and settled back on the beanbag on the floor of her bedroom. I felt so much better. It was me and Iz doing our horoscopes and chatting like we always did. And I had seen the perfect boy. 'Yeah. I've never felt like this before and I just

3

know he's going to feel the same when we meet. Er . . . don't tell anyone though, will you?'

'Course not,' said Izzie. 'Not if you don't want. Your secret is safe with me.'

Tony

'So come on, Tony. Tell us your secret,' begged Robin as we crossed the road outside school. 'I *need* help.'

'No secret,' I said. When we reached the other side, I saw that Annabelle Wilson and her mate Mira Jones were coming towards us on the pavement.

As soon as she spotted us, Mira flicked blond hair back off her face. 'Hi, Tone,' she said in a low voice and gave me a flirty look.

'Hi, girls,' I replied, and gave her a flirty look back (eye contact held a second too long, slightly raised eyebrow and slow smile) then I did the same to Annabelle. She blushed pink. I'd dated both of them last year. Not at the same time. I'd never have got away with it seeing as they're mates. Mira in the winter for six weeks (a record for me as my cut off is usually around four), and Annabelle in the spring for just a few dates. She was sweet but boring after a while. I like a girl who can hold her own in the conversation stakes. Mira was more interesting but she got possessive and I don't do clingy as she found out after yet another 'And where have you been and who with?' conversation.

The girls walked past and Rob and I continued on our way up towards Highgate. Rob turned around.

'They're watching,' he said.

I shrugged and carried on walking. 'Rule number one, my friend, never turn around. Makes you look too keen.'

'Oh right,' said Rob. 'I forgot. Treat 'em mean to keep 'em keen.'

'Ish,' I said. 'You don't have to be mean, just don't look desperate. Girls always want what they can't have. Remember that.'

Rob did a mock salute. 'So come on, Tony, spill. You clearly have the ability to pull any girl you want and I need a few hints.'

'Don't try too hard. Don't do needy.' I didn't know what else to tell him. I've never had to try. Girls like me. Always have, but I don't think it's because of anything I say or don't say, do or don't do. Sometimes I joke around and say I am the Master when it comes to girls but I'm not totally serious. It's simple. I like girls, they like me. Lucky me.

When we got up to Highgate, we went into Costa. We go in most nights after school and always try to bag the stools by the window. That way, we can check out the babes on the street as well as watch the ones inside.

Robin went to get our drinks while I got our places. He's been my mate since I changed schools at the end of last year. Like mine, his family had just moved to the area so he was a newbie too. He's a good guy. On the level. Nice-looking boy, Robin, but no real talent when it comes to pulling. He's always, like, 'Hey, I've got this real cool chat up line, want to hear it?' And I'd go, 'Robin, reality check, man. You don't need a chat up line to get on with girls, you just talk to them like you like them, like you're interested in what they have to say.' Works every time.

Now he reckons he's in love. Hannah is her name. I've never seen him like this over a girl before. He only met her last week when we went bowling. She's OK. Not my type. Bit tomboyish – figure like a boy's too, straight up and down, and she doesn't seem to make much effort with her clothes, she's always in jeans and an old T-shirt. I like girls to look like girls. Especially those with a bit of style about them.

At that moment, Sienna Jeffrey waved from across the street. I waved back. She giggled and headed for the bus stop. About two minutes later, my phone bleeped that I had a text. It was from Sienna. *Wot R U doing Fri pm? XXX*

Rob came back with our cappuccinos and read the text over my shoulder. He sighed. 'Sienna again? Isn't that the hundredth text this week?'

I nodded. 'Might have to change my phone.'

'Just text her back and say, there's a queue and you're way down the line.'

I laughed but I could never be that cruel. Girls have feelings and it's hard letting them down sometimes. We had a snog at a party a few weeks ago and now she thinks that we're an item. But Rob is right. There is a queue. My mobile bleeped that I had another text. This time it was Carrie Johnson. *I know you feel the same way as I do,* she'd written. *'Fraid not,* I thought as I pressed delete, then glanced up to see that Jess Macdonald and Charlotte Rosin were on their way over. Rob perked up immediately as they are two total Barbie babes.

'Don't look so keen, look cool,' I whispered to Rob.

'Aye, aye, Captain,' he said and assumed a bored look and turned to look out the window.

Atta boy, Rob, I thought, *you'll get there in the end.*

Lucy

'I do *not* believe you did that! How could you?'

'I'm sorry, Luce,' said Izzie as we went into assembly on Monday morning. 'It just slipped out.'

I was mad. *Really* mad. Izzie had told Nesta my private business about being in love. 'It was *meant* to be a secret,' I said.

'I know, I know, but we were talking about boys and love and stuff on the phone last night and it just came out.'

Grrrrr, I thought. *GrrrRRRRRRRR.* I wasn't sure if I was more mad that she'd told Nesta my secret or because she'd been having a laugh with her about boys. Having a laugh and chatting about boys was what I did with Izzie. Iz and me. *Me* and Iz. The two of us. *Two.* It was another example of how things were changing with our friendship and I wasn't sure I liked it.

'I don't want her coming with us on our "Find the Mystery Contestant" outings,' I said. We'd agreed two things at the weekend. One was that we were going to refer to the boy as the MC, the Mystery Contestant, and the other was

9

that I needed a plan to meet him. Izzie had suggested that we go up to Highgate and hang out after school every night. It was a good plan. A great plan and I felt excited about it. I could see it in my mind's eye. I'd spot him. He'd see me. He'd feel the connection just like I had when he crossed the road in front of me. Everything would go into slow motion. Sadly the image in my mind's eye kept getting poked out by Nesta. What if he saw her first? I wouldn't stand a chance. She's a boy magnet. She could be a model if she wanted. I'm not even near her league.

'No worries,' said Izzie. 'Nesta's got rehearsals for the school show just about every night.'

'Does she know about the plan?' I asked.

Izzie looked sheepish.

'Izzie!'

Izzie threw up her hands. 'Give her a break, Lucy. She was really pleased you'd seen a boy you liked. And OK, so she knows the plan but she's not going to ruin it for you. She won't be coming with us. She wants to be friends, you know.'

'She wants to be friends with *you*,' I said and then I hated myself for acting like a strop queen. I don't know what's the matter with me lately. Jealous. Moody. Cross! And that can all be in the space of five minutes some days. Not only that, our teacher Wacko Watkins has given us a project – *What Makes Me Me?* It feels like the final straw. Seems everyone in our class has done it no problemo. They all know what they want to do when they leave school, what they're about, what their goals are. Not me though. I don't know who I am, what I want to be or where I fit. The one thing I have ever been

10

sure of in my life was that Izzie Foster was my best friend and now even that isn't a definite any more.

Lucy's diary
24th September

Quelle week *terrible* (to be read in a French accent). Actually, if anyone does read this, I will have to kill them (that's YOU, Lal). Note to self – remember to always lock my diary away after I've written in it, especially after the humungous secret I am about to write in here. Also change the hiding place from under my mattress because I think Lal may have cottoned on to where I've been keeping it and we all know how nosy my dear brother is. Luckily I haven't written too much in it so far, but, now that Izzie isn't as available, I probably will. So, Lal, if you ever find my new hiding place and read it again, you are a dead man and I mean that.

What a week! After three evenings up in Highgate with Izzie, looking for my mystery boy in the cafés, at the bus stops, at the school gates, we were beginning to think that maybe I had dreamed him. We saw boys of every shape and size, but did the MC appear? Not on your nelly, as my gran used to say.

And then . . .

This evening, after checking out the school gates, we headed up to Costa and that's where my life, my dreams, my future were shattered for ever. Just before we got to the café, Nesta appeared. My heart sank because I could see that every boy in the vicinity was checking her out. I thought it was game over for me. If mystery boy saw her, he'd fall in love, think that I was her pet elf (although I think I have grown a quarter of an inch and am now four foot ten and a half!) and that would be it, end of story.

Just as we were about to go into Costa, Nesta took a detour into the newsagent's. Iz and I went to get drinks and scanned the café. So far so good – no sign of my boy.

I looked out of the window in case he was on the street. Suddenly my mouth dropped open. Nesta was coming out of the newsagent's And she wasn't alone. She was with him! *HIM!* My MC!

I could hardly believe my eyes. Iz and I had spent almost a whole week looking for him and, not only had Nesta bumped into him, but in two minutes, *two minutes*, she'd got chatting to him! *Talk about a fast worker*, I thought.

Seconds later, Nesta and his lovely lovelinesss were standing before me. (He was even better-looking close up.) And then Nesta introduced him as her brother, Tony! Brother?!!! I swear my jaw must have hit the floor. It didn't add up. Nesta is dark-skinned. Tony is white. (I was a colour all of my own. Red, red, red.) Turns out he's Nesta's half-brother. Same dad, different mum. Nesta's mum is her dad's second wife. But MY MC IS NESTA'S BROTHER!!!!!!! Ugabugabulah!

And that's when I knew that I could never tell anyone – not Izzie, certainly not Nesta – that Tony was the boy I'd been looking for all week. If he ever found out that I'd been up there looking for him, he'd think I was totally desperate. And if Iz and Nesta found out, it would be a huge laugh for them but utterly humiliating for me.

And then things got even worse – so bad, that I think the tiniest detail of our conversation will be imprinted on my brain for ever. My mind has been replaying and replaying the scene over and over in the fear that I may have given my secret away.

'So. Which one of you is Lucy?' Tony asked.

'I am,' I whispered. I felt wobbly and faint.

'Nesta tells me that you've got your eye on one of the St Michael's boys.' (*Hah! Like, yeah. Like, I have and it's you. Argh!*) 'I go there, so I might know him.' (*Hahahaha. Not. More like double argh!*) 'I'm in Year Twelve. What year is he in? What does he look like?' (*What does he look like? YOU. Argh. Oh! My! God! This is like my worst nightmare. It can't be happening.*)

My cheeks burned furiously. I remember I stuttered something stupid like, 'Er, tall, er . . . hair. He was, um, too far away for me to get a close look.'

And then Izzie piped up: 'Just find us the best-looking boy at your school and that will be him.' (By this time, I think I might have left my body and have been watching the whole scene from the ceiling.)

Tony flashed me a cheeky smile. 'Best-looking boy in the school? But . . . you're looking at him.'

I may have laughed a little too hysterically at this point. *Best-looking boy in the school? I know you are – but do you know I know? Argh. Argh. Argh.*

I couldn't wait to get out of there. What a totally awful outcome, the worst possible. What with Tony asking me to describe the boy and Nesta saying that she reckoned that the reason I hadn't seen the boy was because he might have been doing some extra-curricular class like Tony often did (!!!!), I could not believe that they hadn't twigged that Tony was my MC. It was soooo obvious to me. But it appeared that they hadn't. And now I can never tell Izzie or Nesta and especially not him or he will think I am a sad weirdo. It will have to be my secret for ever.

Tony

'So what do you think of Lucy and Izzie?' asked Nesta when we got on the bus to go home.

'Sweet,' I told her.

'Both of them?'

'Which is which again?'

'Lucy is the blonde one.'

'Yeah. She's a sweet kid. I liked the way she blushed. I like girls who blush. It's cute.'

'Izzie is the taller one. She's got beautiful eyes, hasn't she?'

I laughed. 'Has she now? Can't say I noticed. Nesta, don't even start. Your mates are way too young for me.' Nesta had done this before – when we lived down in Bristol. She was always bringing her friends home from her school who then got a crush on me and she'd get mad at me if I didn't fancy them.

'I wasn't starting anything like that, you dopehead. In fact, if you showed any interest in either Izzie or Lucy, I'd have to kill you. I know what you're like and I don't want to be held

14

responsible for romantic let-downs.'

'No chance, Nesta. Way too young for me. I like girls with a bit of experience.'

'Good, because I want them to like me and I don't want you messing things up by playing with their heads or their hearts.'

'As if. But what do you mean you want them to like you? They're your mates, aren't they? They have to like you. That's the rules. Mates like you.'

'They're *new* mates,' said Nesta. 'Still early days and I'm not sure that Lucy likes me at all. I think Izzie does but Lucy can be a bit aloof some days and I don't know what's going on in her head.'

'She's the blonde one, yeah?'

Nesta nodded. 'Yeah. Like, I've been round her house and met her family, she's got two brothers and we all had a laugh, but then sometimes she goes quiet and I catch her looking at me and . . . I don't know what's she's thinking.'

Tony squeezed my arm. 'Been tough for you, hasn't it, being the newbie?'

'Ish.' She shrugged, then grinned. 'I'll win them over.'

'You always had so many mates round where we used to live,' said Tony. 'Must be hard starting again. It's different with boys. They're not as weird about friendships as girls. Like Rob. We were both newbies, new to the school at least, put on the same footie team. He's a bit of a laugh, he's got a brain so we became mates. End of story. Simple.'

Nesta nodded. 'I was the *only* new girl in our year last term. And yeah, it has been a challenge. Like everyone in our class

15

started together in Year Seven, that's two years they've had together so the friendships have been established. And it's not that anyone's been unfriendly, well . . . except for one girl who's a right cow, Josie Riley.'

'Why's she a cow?'

Nesta wrinkled her nose. 'I bumped into her and her mates in the cloakroom when I first arrived and she put my books in the sink and turned on the taps. When I asked why she'd done that, she said, "Oh, it's an initiation for all new girls," except we both knew that I was the *only* new girl.'

'She's probably jealous, Nesta. You're great-looking and sometimes girls can't handle that. She's threatened.'

'Maybe. She was mean to me when I went to the movies with Iz and Lucy – trying to humiliate us because we couldn't get in. Then some boy she was after made a beeline for me. She didn't like it. She told all of us to stick to Disney – she even said in a loud voice while looking at Lucy, "Anyone can see the midget's underage".'

'Ouch,' I said.

'Yeah. OK, so Lucy looks young but Josie didn't need to say that in front of everyone. She really annoyed me.'

'Sounds to me like she's definitely jealous of all of you. Don't let her get to you.'

'I won't, but girls like her make me realise how important it is to have the *right* mates. Mates who are on my side, who will stick up for me and me for them. Izzie and Lucy stood out straight away as solid as well as fun. I *really* want them to be my mates.'

'No one else?'

'There's a girl called TJ who seems OK but she only hangs out with her mate. Izzie put out the hand to me, if you know what I mean – the hand of friendship. Izzie's really interesting. A bit mad, bit wacky, but I like that. She's into new age stuff like crystals and aromatherapy, I think she even does a bit of witchcraft.'

'What's Lucy like?'

'Lucy? Hmm. She might be small but she's got great style, like she knows how to put an outfit together. And she's funny but . . . solid too. Like you know some girls can be like hyper or giddy, the kind who scream at the slightest thing —'

'Tell me about it,' I said when, as if on cue, a bunch of girls behind us starting screaming with laughter.

'Or bitchy. Some girls can be so bitchy, but Lucy's not like that. She's, yeah, solid but, as I say, not sure she likes me.'

Tony put his hand on mine. 'Who could resist the Nesta Williams charm? She'll come round when she gets to know you better. Invite them over, put out the hand of friendship to her too. It's got to be a two-way thing. In fact, I bet she's a little intimidated. You can be scary, you know.'

'Me? You think?'

'Yeah. You're stunning, you're confident —'

'But I'm not. Not all the time. I just know how to act confident.'

'Well, Lucy doesn't know that. Show her your more vulnerable side.'

'I guess I could invite her over. Her mum has said that she can decorate her bedroom so I could invite her to come and talk décor.'

'Good plan.'

'And you're not going to be home when they come over to ruin it for me?'

'I am *so* not interested, except that if you want these girls as your friends, then I hope it works out. They seemed nice. But I will go out if it makes you feel better.'

'Good. Because the *last* thing I need is one of them falling for you and getting her heart broken.'

Lucy

Lucy's diary
25th September
   Tony is the One.

Tony

Nicky? Annabelle? Janie? Jess? Marie? Bea? Or Tia?

Friday night party at Des's house. Who to take? So many girls, so little time . . .

Lucy

'Nesta's invited us over. You up for it?' asked Izzie. 'Her mum has loads of interior design mags so we can think about how to do your bedroom. Lucy, you there?'

Ohmigod, oh Lordie, oh heckity doodah, I thought. *Nesta's. That means Tony might be there. What shall I wear? Will he be in? How can I make sure I don't blush this time but say something cool and interesting and witty?*

'Lucy?'

'Yeah. Yes,' I replied. 'I'm here. Um, yeah. I'm up for it. Don't think I'm doing anything.'

Tony

I got home around four and could hear that Nesta had some of her mates over. Oops. She'd said that she didn't want me here when they came but I hadn't realised that it was that night. Never mind, too late now I was home. *What were their names again?* I asked myself. *Lizzie and, drat, can't remember the name of the small one who blushed. Shame, because girls like it when you remember their name and I like to impress. Ah well. I'll have to bluff it.*

The voices were coming from . . . hey, blooming cheek! It sounded as if they were in my room. I made my way down the corridor and burst in. It was so funny because the little one was in there with Nesta and she went bright red, like she'd been caught doing something really naughty.

'Just giving Lucy the tour,' said Nesta.

Lucy. Ah, that was her name.

'Only too happy to come home and find pretty girls in my bedroom. Hi, Lucy.'

She went even redder than before. Result! 'Hi,' she replied.

'So how's the search for the mystery man going?' I asked. 'The one with the hair?'

She shuffled about awkwardly and looked at the carpet. 'Er . . . haven't seen him again,' she muttered. She really was painfully shy.

'We need a plan,' said Nesta. 'To get Lucy noticed. You like girls, Tone. What do you look for? What do you find attractive?'

I decided to give Lucy the benefit of some good advice. She was sweet. I'd like to help her find her mystery boy. I gave her my full attention and most charming smile. 'I like girls who are funny. Who make me laugh. And girls who know who they are, what they want and where they're going. Confidence, I suppose. It's a real turn on for boys.'

For some reason, Lucy looked horrified. I even thought for a second that she was going to cry.

'Um, yes . . . er . . . fine,' she stuttered. 'Where's the loo, Nesta?'

Lucy

Lucy's diary

26th September

A total nightmare of a day. I asked Izzie if she fancied Tony. She says she doesn't. Said he's too pretty. Then she asked me if I did. No way, I said, lying.

I went to Nesta's for the first time. She lives in Highgate in a fab garden flat which is so glam with lots of Eastern rugs and rich colours. Fabbie dabbie. Nesta gave me the tour while Izzie sat and read magazines. Tony arrived back and found Nesta and me in his bedroom. It felt weird being in his room looking at his private things and seeing where he sleeps. I was sooooo embarrassed that he would think I was sneaking about in his stuff like some saddo.

He must never ever ever ever find out that he is my MC, otherwise he will think I am desperate and a stalker, but I wonder if it's too late and he already knows – like, he asked if I had seen the mystery boy again and then he gave me a knowing look. Then Nesta asked what Tony wanted in a girl and he blabbed on about confidence and girls that make him laugh, all the time with this big grin on his face and a twinkle in his eye. I swear he was mocking me.

He went out again and then Nesta and Izzie spent the rest of the afternoon going on about how I could get noticed by boys. All I wanted to do was get home and hide under my duvet. I am going to give up on boys. I will never get one. I will never get one like Tony. I think he thinks I am stupid. I am a sad failure, plus I'm not even five foot tall and I have no boobs. Life stinks.

Tony

Nesta's got her mates over again, I thought as I let myself in and heard girls' voices. It was a week since I'd caught Nesta giving Lucy the tour of my room, and, happily for Nesta, she did seem to be getting well in with them. I was glad for her.

I closed the front door quietly and tiptoed over to the door to listen in on their conversation. I wasn't going to go in because I'd promised Nesta that I wouldn't get in the way of her making friends with them. They were talking about snogging. Irresistible not to stay and listen. One of them was talking about snogging a boy who tasted of onions. She hadn't been impressed. Yeah. Quite right. Big mistake. On my list of rules for snogging, fresh breath is a big must. Nesta admitted to snogging seven boys. Wow. *Way to go, sis,* I thought. I knew she'd kissed at least four. I made a mental note to get her to confess all another time.

'How many have you snogged?' I heard Nesta ask. I peeked through the crack of the door to see who she'd asked. She had directed the question to the small one. Lucy. Sweet. She went red.

'None,' she said. 'I've never seen anyone I like.'

'Except mystery boy,' said the dark-haired girl, Izzie. 'Don't forget him.'

Hmm, I wonder who this mystery boy is? I asked myself. *I'm bound to know him if he's at our school.* Izzie had just begun talking about the boys she'd snogged when I had an idea. I opened the door and stood there, hands on hips, tadah! There was that look of horror on Lucy's face again, like when I caught her in my bedroom. I went over and flopped down next to her.

'The art of kissing,' I said. 'My speciality.'

'You wish,' said Nesta. 'You know nothing.'

'I know more than you think, actually,' I said, turning to Lucy. 'Want me to show you how it's done?'

'Tony,' said Nesta in a warning tone.

Little Lucy turned from pink to red to purple. I wished I had a camera.

'Leave her alone,' said Izzie.

'I was just offering to show her how it's done,' I said. 'Then she'll have something to measure it against in the future.'

Lucy giggled.

'Yeah, she'll know what it's like to be kissed by a bigheaded show-off —' Nesta started. 'Go away, Tony.'

I turned to Izzie. 'You want to try?' I asked.

'In your dreams,' she replied. Cheek. She's not my type, so why did I bother wasting the charm on her? *Save it for the ones who respond,* I thought as I turned back to the blusher by my side.

'Lucy. Do you want to learn from the Master?' I asked.

'The Master?' Nesta guffawed.

27

OK, I'll show you girls, I thought. I turned to look at Lucy who looked like she had frozen. I tucked a strand of hair behind her ear, tilted her face up to look at mine. Slowly, slowly does it. No rush, and actually she has a nice face, elfin with pretty blue eyes and a sweet mouth, like a pink flower, and she didn't seem to be objecting now that we were close – in fact, I could see her leaning towards me slightly. She smelled nice too, clean, of apples or some other fruit. I looked deep into her eyes. She looked back and for a second there was a flutter of chemistry. All the better . . .

'Tony!' I heard Nesta say again behind me.

Ha ha. Too late. 'Close your eyes,' I whispered to Lucy. She did as she was told. And then I kissed her. Slow, tender and, actually, nice. Better than I expected and . . . yeah, no doubt about it, she was kissing me back. Very nice. The Master rides again.

Suddenly a hand grabbed the back of my shirt.

'In the kitchen. Now!' Nesta demanded.

I laughed and got up to follow her. Before I went in, I turned back to Lucy. She looked slightly dazed but happy enough, so what was Nesta's problem? I shrugged and gave Lucy a 'What can I do?' look. She shrugged and grinned back. I was beginning to like her. She clearly had a naughty streak.

Hah! I thought as Nesta hauled me into the kitchen. *I don't care what you have to say. Your mate fancies me. I can tell. And I bet that now she's snogged me, that mystery boy she likes will take second place in line behind MOI.*

28

Lucy

Lucy's diary

3rd October

Arrrrrghhhhhhhhh! What is going on? How can life be so good and then so totally crapola? All in the same day? Same hour?

I had my first snog with Tony. OK, so he was messing about, pretending that he was the Master Snogger and offering to show how it was done but when we kissed, it was amazing. I know he felt it too. He must have done. Izzie is always saying that chemistry is a two-way thing and there was definitely some heat when we kissed, hot hot hot, and when he looked into my eyes, oo er, it was meltdown. But then afterwards, I overheard Nesta talking to him in the hall and telling him to stay away from me. Stay away from me? My heart sank. Why did she say that? That's the last thing that I wanted. I really didn't want him to stay away from me. I was happy for him to kiss me and hoped that he would do it again. And again. Very soon. There was only one thing for it. I decided that as soon as Nesta, Izzie and I were on our own, I'd tell them that Tony was my Mystery

Contestant and that I wanted to be kissed by him.

Yeah right, ha ha Lucy Lovering, just shows what a fool you are. How could I have been so stupid as to think that I stood a chance with him? One kiss and I thought we'd be an item. I have been so naive. Any stupid hopes I had were soon dashed because a girl showed up. Not only was she older than me, and taller than me, she was one of the prettiest girls I have ever seen, curvy with long auburn hair. She saw me in the hall when she came in. She kissed Tony then glared at me over his shoulder as if to say, 'Keep away'. He turned and spotted me. I took a step back and he did a little shrug as the girl followed him down the hall into his bedroom.

'Homework,' he said with a cheeky grin before he opened the door and disappeared. I felt like someone had put a knife in me. I was so jealous thinking of their 'homework' and him kissing her instead of me. It really hurt.

Nesta said that she is his new girlfriend. Jessica. New, old, I don't care. Who am I kidding? I do care. I care more than anything. Later Nesta and Izzie started talking about Tony and how no one in their right mind would fancy him because he's so full of himself. Seems like I will never be able to reveal that Tony is the One, my mystery boy, the love of my life.

Tony

'So is it serious with Jess, then?' asked Rob. We were in the Sixth Form recreation room sharing a cheese and tomato sarnie on our lunch break.

I shrugged. 'Dunno. You know me, mate. I'll see how it goes. How you getting on with Hannah?'

'OK . . .'

'Snogged her yet?'

I swear Rob blushed. 'Early days. Didn't want to push my luck.'

'Rob, my man, there's a time to be cool, there's a time to step forward. Don't delay the moment or else it might become awkward.'

Rob nodded. 'Yeah. I was going to do it. Then I wasn't sure she wanted me to.'

I sighed. 'You got to read the signals. Did she lean forward at any time?'

Rob nodded.

'Did she play with her hair, put her hand up to her throat?' I acted out the motions I'd seen girls do a thousand times when they were being coy.

'Yeah. Think so.'

'She wanted you to snog her then,' I said.

'Yeah. I was going to ask her to make sure —'

'Ask her? No. NOOO. *Never* ask a girl if you can kiss her. No. No. They want you to take command. They want you to be a gentleman but they also want you to take charge and, when it comes to kissing, it's not the time to be polite. You have to make them feel like you've been overcome with passion. You can't help yourself. You can't resist.'

Rob laughed. 'What, like, over here, you saucy wench, pucker up.'

I laughed. 'Not exactly. I despair. Rob, you're on your own from now on. And as for Hannah, well, I'll keep my fingers crossed that she takes pity on you.'

Rob chucked the rest of his sarnie at me.

Lucy

Lucy's diary

7th October

Can't stop thinking about Tony and when he kissed me. Was so upset that he has a girlfriend but then Nesta says they rarely last long. Decided that when the going gets tough, the tough need an image overhaul. I've read it in so many mags – that a new image can boost your confidence. So I have decided to change my image and have booked to have my hair cut after school on Thursday.

I am beginning to like Nesta. She's a good laugh and I can see that she's making a real effort to be mates with me as well as Izzie. Not sure whether I can totally trust her with my secret about Tony though. Anyway, I decided to be friendly and made her a halter top. It looks great on her and she was well chuffed.

<u>Things right with my life:</u>

Not a lot but gonna make some changes.

<u>Things wrong and need changing:</u>

I look twelve.

I am a midget. Josie Riley was right.

I am flat-chested but Iz says there are bras even for girls like me with pimples instead of nipples.

I have never had a proper boyfriend and the only boy I like has a gorgeous girl.

Everyone but me knows what they want to do later in life. I don't know who I am, what I want to do or be when I leave school.

Am going to be positive though. Make the changes. Watch out world.

9th October

Arghhhhhhhhhhhhhhh. God, I am sooooooooooooo unhappy. Life is so unfair. I am never ever going out again or at least not for another year at least. My haircut was a major, and I mean *MAJOR*, disaster. Some idiot botched my hair and my new image is now that of a bald chicken with a few wisps on top. Not a good look. All my family stared at me when I got home – even the dogs looked freaked when they saw me. Tony will never fancy me now. Nesta and Izzie took me shopping to get a Wonderbra after my haircut from hell. Not one fitted. Not even the tiniest. I looked like a five-year-old in her mum's bra. I ran out of the mall and went home. Had a good cry for half an hour. And now I am going to cry again . . .

Later

Have done with crying for now because it was giving me a headache. But now I have a swollen face and red eyes as well. And I still have no boobs. Iz and Nesta barged round and gave me an inflatable bra to cheer me up. It was quite funny for a nano-second until I caught sight of my hair in the mirror. I will tell Mum and Dad

34

that I have terrible stomach ache because I really can't ever ever go out again. I have never been so miserable in my whole life.

Still can't stop thinking about Tony. I wonder if he might like a bald girlfriend, just for a change? I wonder if he ever thinks about me and that kiss? It was special, I'm sure it was. Surely he felt it? Although he may well have forgotten about me by the time I face the outside world again, because it will take about a million years to grow my hair back to a point that I can go out without scaring the neighbours.

I am so ugly.

Tony

On the way out of school on Friday night, my mobile bleeped that I had another text. I opened it up and glanced at the message. *Why haven't you called? Mssng U.* It was the fifth from Jess that afternoon. All week she'd been calling or texting, asking what I was doing, where I was going, who I was with. Alarm bells were beginning to ring. I had intended to go and see a movie with her that evening but I was beginning to feel suffocated. I don't like girls checking up on me. I headed home instead, thinking that maybe Nesta's mates would be over and I could see if I could make the cute one blush again. *Yeah, that's what I'll do,* I thought. *And sorry Jess, but you and I are history.*

Lucy

To do list:
    Make Tony fall in love with me.
    Grow a foot taller.
    Redecorate bedroom.
    Get hair fixed.

Tony

To do list:
 Clean football boots.
 Do science homework.
 Tease Nesta's mates.

Lucy

I closed my eyes and prayed that it would be OK as Betty snipped at my hair. I was over at Nesta's.

'Don't worry, Lucy,' said Izzie. 'Least she can't make it worse.'

'Understatement,' I muttered. *Please don't let Tony walk in while I'm having my hair cut,* I added to my prayer. Nesta insisted that I come over when she saw how upset I was about my hair and had talked me into letting Betty, their family hairdresser, try and fix it. I agreed in the end because I knew I couldn't go around looking like a mad person and Mum and Dad hadn't bought the 'I have a terrible stomach ache and can't go out ever again' excuse for a second.

Betty snipped away and the girls made various encouraging noises but I kept my eyes tight shut until it was all over, cut and blow dried.

'Open your eyes now,' said Nesta.

I finally did.

'Wow,' I said. It looked fanbloomintastic. Even I had to admit it. Spiky and short at the front, and she'd even run some white blond highlights through the top. It really suited me.

'You look gorgeous,' said Izzie. 'It shows off your cheekbones.'

I changed my prayer to, *Please God, let Tony walk in now and see me looking so good.* God wasn't listening however because he didn't show. Or maybe he *was* listening and had answered my first prayer to keep Tony away and maybe you only get one prayer answered a day.

For the rest of the evening, we did each other's nails and then flicked through Nesta's mum's interior magazines. I felt so great about everything. I had a new look and soon I'd have a new room to match. And Nesta had been so fab, I was beginning to think that we really could be friends after all and that three wasn't a crowd – three was one more person to share the good times with.

'Nesta,' I asked.

'Yeah . . .'

'Um, you know Tony?'

'Yes.'

'Why doesn't he live with his mum?'

Nesta went quiet. 'She died,' she said after a few moments. 'A road accident when Tony was six months old. A year later, his dad met my mum and so my mum's the only one he's ever really known.'

'Where is he tonight?'

'Some class after school, I expect,' said Nesta.

I shot a look at Izzie. It seemed so obvious to me that Tony was the boy I'd seen and I was amazed that she hadn't put two and two together yet.

She must have finally read my mind because suddenly she clapped her hand over her mouth. 'Ohmigod,' she said. 'OhmiGOD!'

'What?' chorused Nesta and I.

'Tony,' said Izzie. '*Tony*.'

She knew. I *knew* she knew. I went scarlet. She clocked my blushing cheeks and then I knew that she *definitely* knew.

'What?' asked Nesta.

Izzie looked at me as if to say, it's your call. I decided that I would take a risk and trust Nesta.

'Tony,' I said.

'I know,' she said. 'What about him?'

I nodded at Izzie as if to say, 'Feel free to say what you want'. We sometimes had a telepathic thing and she got what I wasn't saying immediately.

'A boy that we didn't see in Highgate because he stays late for classes after school?' said Izzie as she waited for the penny to drop.

Nesta thumped her forehead. 'Oh. Ohhhh! Except we *did* see him! Obvious! Tony is the MC!'

I nodded.

Nesta did a small shriek.

'And he made you kiss him,' giggled Izzie.

'I really didn't mind,' I said.

'And I told him to stay away from you,' said Nesta. 'You must have hated me.'

'Not as much as I hated that red-haired girl. Jezebel.'

'Why didn't you say, Lucy?' asked Nesta.

'I was afraid you'd tell him and I'd look like such a saddo.'

At that second, we heard someone in the hall. Moments later, Tony appeared.

Tony

As I put my key in the front door and went into the hall, I could hear that Nesta's mates were round again. I followed the voices into our living room where they were lounging about on the sofas. The little one, Lucy, looked as if she'd had her hair cut. She looked good, like a cheeky cherub. She blushed when she saw me.

'Hi everyone,' I said and turned to Lucy. 'You look great.' I went and sat next to her. 'Want another kissing lesson?'

Lucy looked at the floor and then at Nesta and then at Izzie.

Nesta looked at Izzie.

Izzie looked at me.

Nesta looked at me.

Lucy looked up at the girls, glanced at me, looked at the floor again. They all looked very shifty, like I'd caught them doing something that they shouldn't be doing. And Nesta wasn't hauling me away from her mate as I expected. She and

Izzie were staring at me like I had egg on my face. I checked my flies. No, they were done up, so what was going on?

'What?' I asked. 'Why are you staring?'

Lucy starting giggling and soon Izzie joined in and then Nesta. Maybe I had a chocolate moustache from the cappuccino I had on the way home in Costa. Jeez, that would be embarrassing. *Better go and check in the mirror,* I told myself. I got up to go into the hall. The girls were near to hysterical, shoulders shaking, Nesta even had tears of laughter in her eyes. Whatever they were laughing at, I couldn't see it, and I think it's mean to exclude people when you're having a good joke.

'Girls,' I said. 'Sometimes you can be *really* juvenile.'

'I thought you liked girls with a sense of humour,' Lucy was saying as I shut the door behind me.

Hmm, she's not as shy as I thought she was, I told myself.

'Not when it's directed at him,' I heard Nesta say. I put my ear to the door. 'And I won't say anything about, you know,' I strained to hear, 'about him being the MC, if you don't want.'

MC. MC? What did she mean? I wondered. Then I twigged. *MC. Mystery Contestant. That's what they called the boy Lucy fancies. Hey! Wait a minute. So that was it! Blimey. I* am *the boy she fancies. It's me. I put my ear back to the door. Pff. I should have realised. It was obvious really. Best-looking boy in the school. That's me, and not because I'm vain – loads of girls have said I am.*

'Thanks,' Lucy said behind the door. 'I don't want.'

Well, well! I thought. *Don't worry, Lucy, your secret is safe with me. Hah! No wonder she had that naughty look on her face after I'd kissed her. She was probably thinking she was the only one who knew her secret. Well, she was then. But now we all know. Except . . . yeah, no one knows that I know. No one knows that it's my secret too. Hah! That will be my secret.*

'Anyway,' said Izzie. 'I reckon you could get anyone you want looking the way you do now. Play the field for a while.'

'Ah, but I have been kissed by the Master,' said Lucy, giggling again.

Yeah, you have, my little munchkin, I thought. *And don't you forget it. So I am the MC. I swear to myself that I will never let on that I know the secret but . . . that doesn't mean I can't have some fun with it.* I went to my room to call Jess and think over this latest round of developments. As Rob would say, another one bites the dust.

Lucy

'I *love* your outfit,' said Nesta when we met up outside the hall ready to go into the Clothes Show Live.

'Thanks,' I said. We had all agreed to make an effort for the event and I was pleased with what I was wearing because I had made it myself. A grey crepe wrap-over skirt and a halter-neck made from pale blue sari material left over from my room redecoration. Nesta was wearing black leather trousers, the red halter-top I had made her and a little jacket, and Izzie had on a hippie dippie outfit in purple with some great amethyst jewellery. I reckoned we looked the business.

Inside, the hall was heaving and, after we'd paid our entrance fee, we launched ourselves straight in and had a fab time cruising around the stalls, trying clothes on, and Nesta was even stopped by a model scout who gave her a card and asked her to get in touch.

As we left one stall, I noticed a group of girls from our school surrounding a boy. I could see that he was lapping up the attention and for a moment, I felt a stab of jealousy. It was Tony. Worse still, one of the girls was Josie Riley. She was flicking her hair, looking deeply into his eyes, doing all the flirty-gerty stuff. Nesta must have noticed my face fall. She linked arms.

'Don't worry, Lucy. He may be a flirt but he's not stupid.'

I wasn't so sure. He'd said that he liked confident girls and Josie was certainly that. But watching him made me think. *He must have girls swarming around him like that all the time. Well, I'm not going to be one of them.* Watching him lapping up the attention gave me a big lesson in love. *I am not going to fall at his feet like the others,* I decided. *I may still love him but I am going to play it oh so cool.*

Suddenly Josie spotted us and gave us a false smile and a wave.

'Want to go over?' asked Nesta.

I darted behind a clothes rail. 'No way,' I said. 'I couldn't bear it if he likes her.'

'OK,' said Nesta. 'And don't worry, he hasn't seen us.'

The hours flew by as we tried on more clothes and sampled every beauty product on offer. Izzie went off to buy a toe ring and Nesta and I decided to go and watch a catwalk show. We set off in the direction of the show, turned a corner and I walked smack into Josie.

'Ah, the midget,' she said and then looked at my halter-top. 'And what have you got on? The Eastern look was out years ago.'

Her friends started laughing behind her.

'She made those clothes herself and I think she looks

fantastic,' said Nesta. 'I don't suppose someone with your IQ could even sew on a button.'

It was awful. I hate it when people argue. It was good of Nesta to come to my defence but the two of them were squaring up like ready for a fight. And then Josie purposely stood on Nesta's foot. I saw Nesta wince. Josie was wearing spiky heels.

'Oi,' I started.

'Oh *sorry*,' said Josie insincerely. 'Did that hurt, Nesta?'

'Need a hand?' asked a male voice.

We all turned. It was Tony.

'No, I'm fine,' said Josie going girlie and coy.

He brushed her aside. 'Not you,' he said and put his arm around Nesta. 'You OK?'

Josie looked shocked. 'We were just admiring Lucy's outfit,' she said and her friends started sniggering behind her.

Tony turned to me. 'Yeah. Me too,' he said and he sounded like he meant it. 'Looking good, kiddo. Come on, girls, I'll buy you a cappuccino.'

Josie clearly thought he meant her too and trooped along behind us.

Tony put one arm around Nesta and the other around me and marched us away. *Ha ha. That showed her*, I thought as she sloped off.

'I thought you liked girls who were confident,' I said.

'Do me a favour,' he said. 'I like the music turned up but not that loud, if you get my meaning.' And then he looked deeply into my eyes and I swear I heard the sound of violins fill the hall.

Hold on, there actually *were* violins . . .

The catwalk show had started at the other end of the hall –

laser lights were flashing and the models began to strut their stuff down the catwalk.

'I need a drink,' said Nesta. 'Can we see the show later?'

I nodded.

Tony looked torn between staying with us and going to watch the show.

'Oh go and watch the girls. That's what you came here for,' said Nesta. 'We'll catch you later.'

Tony grinned, gave us the thumbs up and set off towards the back of the hall while Nesta and I made our way over to the nearest coffee stall and took our places in the queue. She looked shaken and leaned against a wall.

'You OK?' I asked.

She reached down and rubbed her foot. 'That really hurt,' she said. 'I didn't want to say how much. Tony can be very protective of me – if he knew that she was the girl who made my life so miserable when I first arrived at school, he might have really given her a hard time.'

'What do you mean?' I asked.

'Oh, she pushed me about one day in the cloakrooms, called me names, poured water on my books.' Nesta shrugged one shoulder as if to say it didn't matter, but I could see that just the memory of it made her eyes glisten.

I linked my arm through hers. 'Well, Josie has always been mean. I wouldn't take it personally. She's horrible to me too. Remember she calls me a midget all the time.'

Nesta nodded. 'You may be small but you're perfectly formed.'

'Exactly,' I said. 'And anyway, Nesta, you've got me and

Izzie now. We'll look after you.'

Nesta's eyes filled up even more. 'Have I? Really? Because I thought you didn't like me at first.'

'I was jealous,' I admitted. 'I thought I was losing Izzie but I am sorry – I know now that you weren't out to steal her from me. And I'm sorry that I wasn't more welcoming. I was a cow. It can't be easy starting a new school late.'

Nesta rolled her eyes. 'Tell me about it.'

I laughed. 'Tell you about me being a cow or it being hard starting school late?'

Nesta laughed too. 'Er . . . both. Start with you being a cow.'

In that instant, I knew that we were going to be mates, really good mates from then on. I was about to ask her more about Josie when a woman behind us tapped me on the shoulder. I turned to see what she wanted.

'Where did you get your top?' she asked.

'Oh, I made it.'

'Really? Good for you,' she said. 'I'm impressed.'

'She made this as well,' said Nesta, doing a twirl for her.

'I like doing halters,' I told her. 'They're easy to make.'

'You've got a good eye,' smiled the woman. 'A simple design but well cut. Well done.' She put her hand in her bag, produced a card and handed it to me. 'Here. Remember me when you've finished fashion college.'

'Fashion college?'

'Yes. I presume you're going to do fashion?'

It was like a light went on in my head. Ping! Of course. It was obvious. My way was clear. Fashion!

I nodded. 'Yes. I am. Course I am.'

'Well, good luck and get in touch when you've finished. I am always looking for fresh talent and innovative design and if you carry on like this, you've got a good future in front of you.'

She saw someone she knew at the end of the coffee queue and went back to join them. Nesta took the card.

'Ohmigod,' she said.

'What?' I asked.

'That was Viv Purcell.'

The name meant nothing to me.

'*The* Viv Purcell. She's only one of hippest designers there is. Mum did a whole feature on her on the news one night last week. She is Big with a capital B.'

I felt myself glowing with pleasure. Not only had she picked me out but she was dead on – a designer, that's what I wanted to be. That is what I *was*. I could feel happiness flooding through me. I had not one, but two great mates. I had a career in front of me. I felt like doing cartwheels. In fact, if I'd been wearing trousers, I would have done!

Tony

I left the Clothes Show early and went to Rob's house to watch a movie he'd been raving about.

When I got home, I was about to go into my room when I saw Lucy coming out of the bathroom. She was beginning to grow on me and it had been fun hanging out with her, Nesta and Izzie at the show.

'Pst, Lucy,' I said. 'In here.'

She looked up and down the corridor, probably looking for my parents, but, seeing no one, she followed me into my room.

I knew she would.

I shut the door, went straight over, put her arms around my neck and kissed her. She didn't resist.

I knew she wouldn't.

'So do you want go out some time?' I asked when we came up for air. A date or two, that would be all, but she was cute, it would be fun and it was flattering to be adored the way that she clearly adored me. I was her MC. Her meestery contestant.

I knew her secret.

Then, blow me down. She gave me a really slow up and down look as if she was sizing me up. Then she stuck her bottom lip out, pouted and said, 'I don't know. I'll . . . think about it.'

Holy moley and flipping heck, I thought. *Girls don't turn the Master down. What's going on?*

I gave her my killer-watt smile. 'Suit yourself,' I said. 'You're probably too young for me anyway.'

She laughed, opened the door . . . and left!

I gave her a few seconds. She'd be back. Girls always came back for more.

She didn't.

I stuck my head out into the corridor. No sign of her.

And then I laughed too. She was cool. *So . . . you want to play, do you, Lucy Lovering? I thought. OK, let game commence.*

Lucy

'Lucy,' said Nesta in a mega-loud voice. 'I want to look at some aromatherapy oils.'

We were at Camden Market on Saturday afternoon doing some early Christmas shopping and Izzie had seen a boy that she really liked. He was manning a stall selling oils and Izzie was too shy to go and talk to him. Of course, Nesta was having none of that and dragged us back over to the stall. It wasn't long before Izzie got chatting to him because she's into all that New Age stuff and knows a lot about essential oils. Nesta and I decided to leave them to it.

We had a look at a few of the shops on the ground floor then Nesta went off to find a Ladies so I cruised around on my own. After a while I got the feeling that I was being watched. I turned around and saw someone dart behind a stall. *Probably Nesta being stupid,* I thought as I carried on my way. In the next aisle, I got the same feeling and turned again. Once again, someone darted away. I was sure it wasn't Nesta this time. I got the impression that it was a boy because I saw jeans and Converse sneakers before he disappeared from view. I turned into the next aisle and hurried along. I glanced over my shoulder, ducked into a stall and hid behind a curtain in the changing room ready to ambush the boy.

'You all right, love?' asked the stall owner.

'Er . . . yes,' I whispered. As I spoke I spotted a pair of Converse sneakers appear under the curtain on the other side to where I was hiding. I sprang out to surprise my stalker.

Tony leaped back as I pounced on him. 'Wargh!'

'So it was you!' I accused.

'Me what?'

'Following me.'

He grinned, nodded and then turned to the stall owner. 'Sorry. Has my patient been causing trouble?'

The stall lady looked puzzled. 'No. Not at all.'

'Come on, Lucinda,' said Tony. 'Time to take your medication.'

I laughed as he took my arm and hauled me along the aisle. He looked back at the stall. 'She goes loopy if I don't look after her.'

The stall lady rolled her eyes. 'Yeah right,' she said. 'Think it might be you who needs the medication, dear.'

I laughed. 'Hah!' I said. 'She had your number.' Then I punched his arm gently. 'So why were you following me?'

Tony put his hand on his heart. 'For my heart is smitten by thy fair face and thou doth pull at my heartstrings like a magnet.'

'You don't half talk tosh,' I said, but I was pleased to see him. It seemed like ages since we'd bumped into each other at Nesta's.

I'd seen him a couple of times since I had confessed to the girls that he was my MC. I still wasn't sure what he thought of me though. One time, he was really cool so the next time when he was more flirty, I out-cooled him. After that, every time I went over, he wasn't there and Nesta had started hanging out at my house more and more. In the meantime, I had decided that being cool all the time didn't get much of a result so the next time I saw him, I was going to be warmer.

'So. Drink, madam?' asked Tony.

'Don't mind if I do,' I replied with what I hoped was a flirty smile. 'In fact, I said I'd meet Nesta at the juice stall in about ten minutes.'

We went and sat at a table near the canal and Tony bought us two apple-and-carrot juices, which were yummy. It felt great to be sitting with him and I noticed a few girls go by and check him out and then look at me. I straightened my back and attempted to look like it was completely possible that I might be his girlfriend. *Some chance,* I thought, *he is so gorgeous. He would never be with a girl like me for real.*

'So, Juicy Lucy,' he said after he'd drained his glass. 'Fancy going to a movie next week?'

'Splurgh . . .' I had just taken a big slurp of juice and was so surprised by his question that I choked on it and then had to cough like mad because it went down the wrong way.

Tony grinned. 'I'll take that as a yes then,' he said.

Cheek. He's so confident, I thought, but I couldn't resist nodding that it was a yes. In fact, it was a double yes with knobs on.

Tony

'Nesta, get off my case, OK?' I said. 'I thought you'd have been pleased that I am hanging out with your mate. *She* seems happy enough about it.' It had been a couple of weeks since I'd bumped into Lucy at Camden and I was getting to like her more and more.

We'd been to see a movie together. I'd picked one I knew she'd like, a romantic comedy, and her behaviour while we were watching it had made me smile. She acted like she was trying to be all grown up and had sat with a straight back throughout the film. She'd almost jumped out of her skin when our hands brushed each other when we both reached into the popcorn at the same time. Her shyness is so cute.

We'd also been for smoothies in Highgate last weekend and that time she was more confident. She'd been working on some dress designs and was animated about her ideas. I told her that her passion was very alluring and she went bright pink, but I could see she was chuffed as anything. Apart from that, we'd hung out after school in Costa, casual, but I made sure I sat near her and made a lot of eye contact. Heh heh, all part of the master plan to get her to fall into my arms.

Nesta grimaced. 'I mean it, Tony. If you hurt her, I will kill you. Personally. Lucy's a sweet girl and we're really getting along now. The last thing I need is for her to get messed up with you and then feel that she has to avoid me as well as you.'

'I am not going to ruin it for you. I know your motto: boys come and go, friends are for life. Listen, if anything it's her that's giving me the run around!'

'Yeah right,' said Nesta. 'When has a girl ever given you the run around?'

'No really. She really is. It's hysterical, sometimes she's pleased to see me and her face lights up; other times, like the other night at Costa, she's, like, "Whatever," and goes home early. Early! Like she has something better to do!'

Nesta started laughing. 'Good for her,' she said.

'For her maybe. Not for me. Sometimes I call and she says, "Oh hi, Tone, call you back in a mo," and then she doesn't. So I call her and she goes, "Oh, sorry, meant to call. Forgot." *Forgot?* I mean, as you well know, girls do *not* treat *me* like that. There is a queue of girls hoping that I will call them. So chill, Nesta. *She's* giving *me* the run around.'

'I have trained her well,' said Nesta in the voice of Obi-Wan Kenobi from *Star Wars*.

'No,' I said. 'Oh *no*. Don't tell me that you've been giving her advice about dealing with me.'

'Not about you, dingbat. About boys in general. Course I have. She's my mate and you know it is my area of expertise.'

I thumped my forehead with my hand. 'And who trained you up? *Moi.*'

Nesta grinned. 'Yeah. So you only have yourself to blame.' She scrutinised me closely. 'Sure you're not playing with her? Like she's a pet or something?'

I shrugged. 'Bit. I mean, we're young, we're free, etc, etc. But I do like her. I do. And while we're on the subject of Lucy, tell me, what does she say about me? Does she talk about me? I bet she can't stop talking about me, yeah? Always asking questions? Trying to get everything she can out about me from you?'

Nesta shook her head. 'Actually no. She never asks about you. Dunno. Maybe because you're my brother. Maybe she talks to Izzie.'

'Huh.' *She might be playing it cool,* I thought, *but she's good, really good. Almost as good as I am. Drat and double drat.*

Nesta got up and left the kitchen, leaving me alone with my thoughts. I made a second cappuccino and sat at the breakfast bar. *I might call Lucy and see what she's doing,* I decided. I hadn't told Nesta the whole truth and that was that Lucy was starting to get under my skin in a way that no other girl ever had before. No one was more surprised about it than me, but when we were together, it felt right. We fitted. It felt comfortable, like I'd known her for ever, but more than that – and something I hadn't told Nesta in case she whacked me one – there was some almighty chemistry going on between us. It was there the first time we kissed, but I was messing about then, trying to freak out Nesta. Now we'd had a couple of sessions, it was getting steamy – but it wasn't just that, I'd had plenty of steam with other girls. Lucy was interesting, fun to be with, she had ambitions and we had a laugh. So yeah, I fancied Lucy more than I had let on to anyone, even Rob.

I wondered what she thought now that we'd had a few dates. Did she still rate me as her perfect boy? Had I lived up to the expectations she had when she first saw me and came looking for me as her Mystery Contestant? Of course, I could never ask or let on that I knew that I was the boy she was looking for. That was still my secret. I hadn't told Rob about that either.

Yeah. Lucy was different and she was a challenge. Just thinking about kissing her was making me feel hot and bothered. Time to take it all to another level methinks. So far, we'd only kissed, but last night when the girls had a sleepover here, Lucy came into my room and we had a long snog on my bed before she went in to share the sofa-bed with Izzie in Dad's office. I tested the water about going a step further and she brushed me off which I expected first time around, but she didn't seem mad with me, so . . . maybe next time I'll try again and see what happens. I know she wants me.

I was about to call her when my mobile rang. Telepathy. It was Lucy.

'Hey Tone,' she started.

'Hey Juicy Lucy. You were gone by the time I got up this morning. I thought I'd see you after the sleepover.'

'Um yeah. Stuff to do. Listen. Um. We need to talk.'

Oh God, I thought. *The 'we need to talk' line. It usually comes when a girl wants to tie me down. So maybe she's going to prove me wrong after all, she's not as laid back as I thought and she's going to*

do the clingy, 'Are we really committed? Are we an item?'
conversation. Maybe it's not such a bad thing. Maybe, yes . . . maybe
this time I could actually commit. Well, for a few weeks at least.

'OK, shoot.'

'I . . . er . . .'

Spit it out, I thought. *I've heard it all before. You want*
commitment. You want people to know we're a couple. Etc, etc.
Weirdly the idea of being with one girl for a while wasn't
freaking me out like it usually did.

'OK, I'll just dive in. I . . . um . . . It doesn't feel right any
more.'

'Doesn't feel right? Wha—'

'Let me finish. You know I really like you but I've been
feeling miserable after last night after the . . . um, snog sesh.
I'm not ready to go further, Tony. I want it to be special and
I'm not sure of you or us yet.'

Oh here we go, I thought. *She's going to ask me to go steady or*
whatever it's called. I can do that if that's what she wants.

'So . . .' She hesitated.

'Yes?'

'So I don't think we should date any more. I . . . I hope we
can stay friends.'

WHAT?! I thought. *Am I hearing what I think I'm hearing?*
Those are all my lines. I hope we can stay friends. It's over. I really
like you but . . . Myyyy lines. MY lines! 'What?'

'I know there's something special with us but . . . it's all
been happening a bit fast and I feel bad about doing this on
the phone but I didn't want to leave things unclear any longer.
After last night, I think it's obvious that you want to take

things further – and why not, you are older than me – but I'm not ready so I think it's for the best if we take a break.'

A girl was dumping me. Dumping *me*! This just *didn't* happen.

'Maybe we can do a movie or something some day, hey?' she continued. (*Also* one of my lines) 'Be nice to see you sometimes. I don't want to lose touch.' (Don't want to lose touch! *Another* of my lines.) 'Tony. Tony. Are you there? You've gone very quiet.'

I told myself to put up the inner barriers fast, to not let her know what I was feeling. But what *was* I feeling? Being dumped was new territory to me. I took a breath. 'Yeah I'm here. Sorry, babe. A text was coming in.' (Big lie but I have to bluff it.) 'From Jess. Remember her? You met her in the hall a while back. So yeah. What were you saying? Take a break? Yeah. Good idea. Absolutely cool with me. We weren't exactly an item, were we?'

'No but —'

'No buts, babe. Stay cool yeah.'

'Yeah.'

'Laters.'

I put the phone down. Dumped! Me! I could not believe it. First time in my life and by a girl a lot younger than me, mate of my sister's too. What was I feeling? Stunned. Surprised. And what's more . . . hurt.

Lucy

Lucy's diary

15 December

Oh my God. What have I done? Have I just made the biggest mistake of my whole life? Argh and ergh. I have just finished with Tony. Why did I do that? I love him. Have I blown it for ever just because he wanted to go further and I panicked? Oh cripes. He must think I am such a big baby. What now? Go crawling back? Beg? No way, he'd love that. Oh heckity heck. I hate all this game playing. I don't want to do it but maybe have to with a boy like him. I can't let him see how he gets to me. I shall be cool. I shall, I can do it. I shall be glacial. I shall be a lofty goddess looking down on the Tonester from afar. He is the one who will come crawling back. Oh Goooood. I think I am going to blub.

30th March

Keep forgetting to write this! Weeks and weeks have gone by and I have been a very good girl and totally focused on my school work.

I think for the first time in my whole life I am actually up to date with homework and even ahead with my art project. Mum has been very worried and thinks I am ill. I probably am – lovesick – but I had to do something to take my mind off Tony and the fact that I may have lost him for ever.

Everyone seems to have a boy, though. Izzie has a new boyfriend called Ben. He sings in a band called King Noz and is v. cool. I like him better than the other boy she was after for a while. He was called Mark and was a bit full of himself methinks. Izzie likes Ben better too. She's going to sing with him next time the band performs.

Nesta has met a new boy called Simon Pedington Lee. *Très* posh. He lives in a big house in Holland Park. She's been a bit weird since she met him, not like her usual confident self, which is strange because usually no one phases Nesta, but Simon's sister and her mate have intimidated her for some reason. I think it maybe because they are well loaded – like mega doshed up.

I am the only singleton still. So much for my lofty goddess act. Sometimes I really regret that I ended things with Tony. Specially when my mates are out with their boys and I have no one to hang out with. Boo hoo blub blub. No, actually I am OK. I had hoped that I'd meet someone else though cos part of the reason I broke up with Tony was that I wanted to date a few more boys and see how they compared. He was my first snog. Nesta's always saying: so many boys, so little time. So where are they all? That's what I'd like to know.

Nesta was so funny after I'd finished with Tone. She was so apologetic. He'd told her that *he'd* finished with me. Cheek of it! But I could never tell her the real reason that I wasn't seeing him any more. She'd have killed him. I saw him a few weeks later over at her house and confronted him. He smiled and said, 'Everyone has their own version of events.' I swear he looked sad when he said it. Ah well. What can you do when your life's full of poo? I'm a poet and I don't know it.

Nesta told me last week that Tony has a new girlfriend. Felt jealous. I wonder if she puts out. I am not going to think about him any more. Instead I will find a boy and make *him* jealous and see how Tony likes it.

That's it. Goodnight, ta ta and toodleoo.

Tony

I had an almighty hangover. *Never again,* I thought as I staggered out of bed and out towards the kitchen. I'd spent the previous evening with Anna, a girl I've been out with a few times. I doubt if it's going to last though. I don't feel like being tied down now or anytime soon. *God, my mouth is dry,* I thought, *and my head's pounding like a bunch of goblins are Riverdancing in steel boots on my brain. Must have coffee, must have coffee.*

'Whoa!' I said when Lucy, Izzie and Nesta burst out laughing as I opened the door into the kitchen. 'Er . . . whoops!' I was only wearing my boxers. I put my hands over my crotch and I sort of hopped out of the room backwards. 'Nesta, why didn't you tell me you had guests?'

'And risk the wrath of the zomboid one by waking you up early on a Sunday? I don't *think* so,' she replied.

What did I do to deserve an annoying sister like Nesta? I asked myself as I legged it back to my room and looked at my reflection in the mirror. I had bed hair! What would Lucy think?! It was sticking out in all directions. I dashed into the bathroom and had a quick shower. When I'd finished, I slicked my hair back with a touch of gel and sloshed on some of Dad's Armani aftershave which I nicked for special dates and I know is one of Lucy's favourites. *Oops.* I checked myself. *Would she think I was trying too hard? Too late. The deed is done.* I tried to wipe the hair gel off so it wouldn't look too obvious, then I went and put on my best black jeans and T-shirt. They're a good combo. Casual but look the biz. When I was presentable, I tiptoed back along the corridor and listened at the door for a moment, just in case there were any more interesting confessions going on. *Hmm, singing? Someone was singing. Not Nesta. She can't sing for toffee.*

I poked my head around the door. 'Hey, who was that singing?'

'It was Izzie,' said Lucy.

'Wow, you've got a good voice,' I said.

Izzie looked chuffed.

I grabbed myself a coffee and hung about for a while, but the girls seemed to be occupied. A power breakfast or something girlie like that. I was glad to see Nesta with Izzie and Lucy and acting more like her usual self. Lately she'd been hanging out with her new bloke Simon and his sister Tanya and her mate Cressida who is way stuck up. I went horse-riding with them all one day and didn't like the way the girls looked down their noses at my sis. Simon's cool though so I didn't say anything. I made myself useful by making toast and coffee and I tried to catch Lucy's eye but she was acting like I wasn't there. Very frustrating. I ate my toast nonchalantly like I couldn't care about her either. *Enough,* I thought when after my third bagel she hadn't even glanced at me. *No one ignores the Master. There's a time to be cool, there's a time to get noticed,* I thought. *It's time to turn on the charm.* I went and stood right in front of her so she had to look at me. We were eyeball to eyeball and yes, the old chemistry was still there, no mistake.

'I suppose a snog is out of the question?' I asked in a posh voice.

I knew that would do it. She burst out laughing. *Result,* I thought. *Now I can leave.* And I did.

Always leave 'em wanting more.

Lucy

It was Izzie's big night. The night she was going to sing in public for the first time with King Noz. I found her doing her make-up in the cloakroom at the back of the pub where the gig was being held in Kentish Town. She looked amazing, like an alien rock chick in a short black dress matched with some wild accessories: turquoise gauntlets, blue furry leggings and an amazing blue perspex choker with spikes on it. She was doing her eye make-up silver and was adding silver false eyelashes to complete the look.

'You OK?' I asked.

'I am *so* nervous,' she said then looked towards the door. 'Is Nesta OK out there?'

'Yeah, think so. Don't be nervous. You look fantastic,' I said.

'Thanks. Sure she's OK?'

'She was chatting to Simon at the bar. She seemed OK. Why?'

'I caught her in here crying before.'

'Nesta – crying! Why? What's happened?'

'She was in the loo and Simon's sister and her mate came in and didn't realise that anyone was in one of the cubicles and they started talking about her. One of them, the stuck-up one —'

'Cressida.'

'Yeah. She said that she thought that Simon was only going out with her to shock his mum and dad.'

'But why would Nesta shock them?'

'Because she's mixed race.'

'But that's ridiculous,' I said. 'I was talking to Simon before. I can tell he genuinely likes her.'

Izzie nodded. 'We know that but there are still some totally ignorant people on the planet. And then she called Nesta a zebra.'

'A zebra? Why?'

'Half black, half white.'

'Jeez. That's so mean.'

Izzie nodded. 'It really upset Nesta. She lets those girls get right under her skin.'

I made my way to the door. 'I'll go and find her and I'll give those stupid girls a piece of my mind too.'

'I think it's only Cressida who's bitchy. Nesta said Simon's sister, Tanya, stood up for her. I wish she'd just not hang out with them. She's been acting weird since she met them, like she has something to prove. We're her real mates, can't she see that?'

'I know.' I made a fist. 'Mess with my mate, you mess with me,' I said.

Izzie grimaced. 'Yeah, all four foot ten of you.'

'And a half,' I replied. 'I have grown.'

When I got back into the hall, I saw Nesta disappearing out of the door of the back of the hall with Tanya. She saw me and gave me a wave. A moment later, Tony came in the front of the hall. I could see Cressida clocked him right away but he walked straight towards me. Nesta had said something about Cressida fancying Tony and trying to get off with him when they had all gone horseriding. I had been about to follow Nesta out, but then thought, *I'll show you*. Tony asked if I wanted to dance. I said yes – I wasn't in the mood to be coy and he had asked for a snog the last time I saw him so I followed him on to the dance floor. The first band of the evening were playing and they weren't bad. Easy music to dance to and it felt great to have an excuse to be so close to Tony again. He smelled lovely, Armani. I know he nicks his dad's but it suits him – some aftershaves are well overpowering but that one is subtle. I nuzzled into his neck and inhaled the scent mixed with his own and, as he moved closer in, I felt myself starting to melt into him. So comfy to be near him. Felt so right. When the song had finished, we both pulled away and the expression in Tony's eyes made me want to put my arms round him and kiss him, right there in front of everyone. I took a deep breath. *I am a glacial goddess,* I thought as I felt heat rise up to my cheeks.

'Laters,' I said.

'Laters,' said Tony in a suggestive voice.

I took a few more deep breaths, turned away and went to do a last check on Izzie. She looked pale.

'It's going to be OK,' I said. 'You look fab. You have a great voice. Just relax and go for it.'

Izzie nodded and Ben took her hand and led her towards the stage wings ready for their performance. I gave her the thumbs up. I really felt for her.

Back in the hall, Nesta had reappeared so I went straight over to her.

'Izzie told me what Cressida said about you. What a cow.'

Nesta giggled. 'I'm a zebra, she's a cow. I told her that Tony fancied you and she was like, "Er, I doubt it. Like, not when he could have me".'

'Oh really,' I said.

I glanced around and could see Tony at the back of the hall chatting with Simon. I went over to him. By now, Cressida had joined them and was doing a flick-flicky thing with her hair and looking meaningfully into Tony's eyes. He looked like he wanted to get away. I went and stood beside him and slipped my hand into his.

'Want another dance?' I asked, standing in front of Cressida.

He nodded eagerly and led me towards the dance floor. 'Thanks. That girl is scary.'

Once on the dance floor, I glanced at Cressida. She was watching us through narrowed eyes. I remembered what she'd said about Nesta, snuggled into Tony and put my arms around his neck and thought, *And it's goodbye to me being a glacial goddess.* 'Remember that snog you wanted the other day?' I asked.

He laughed, nodded and we leaned towards each other and went for it. A really long smoochy snog. I opened my eyes and looked over Tony's shoulder. Cressida's jaw had fallen open. *Serves you right for slagging off my mate,* I thought as I closed my eyes again and let myself forget everything except the sensation of being close to Tony and being wrapped in his arms. It felt utterly delicious and I wanted the moment to never end.

Our cosy bubble was interrupted when the first band finished and the lights came on up on the stage. Tony and I drew apart and clapped loudly while I tried to catch Izzie's eye as she went to take her place at the microphone. She was looking at the stage floor and still looked terrified. Ben took his place centre stage and played the opening chords; behind him, the rest of the band began to play and then Izzie joined in with her lovely velvet voice. As the song progressed, I could see that she was beginning to relax so I relaxed too. Tony stood behind me so that I could lean back on him, with his arms around my waist – lovely.

I glanced around the hall. People seemed to be enjoying the set. And then Nesta marched out into the middle of the dance floor and began dancing – not just swaying to the music like other people were doing around the edges of the hall. She was giving it her all, disco dancing a go go like she'd had too much caffeine. I felt Tony take his arms away from my waist. A few people were laughing, a lot of people were watching and the band were staring at her with disbelief. *What the heck is she doing?* I thought. I looked around at Tony. He held his hands up as if to ask the same question. Izzie looked bewildered and I started to feel angry. Nesta was stealing the limelight. It was Izzie's show. Not hers. I dashed on to the dance floor.

'Nesta, go and sit down!'

'Why? Trying to gereveryone dancing,' she slurred. Her

breath stank of alcohol.

Oh God, she's drunk, I thought with horror. 'Everyone's *looking* at you,' I said.

'S'all right. Un showing en how isdone.'

I grabbed her wrist firmly and pulled her to the side of the dance floor. 'It's Izzie's moment. Not yours,' I whispered. 'Have you been drinking?'

Nesta nodded. 'Snice. Tanyannme. Champy-ain.'

Behind me, the band had carried on and people were watching them again, apart from Tony who came straight over. He helped me to get her to a chair. The moment she sat down, she slumped forward and rested her head on the table.

'She's drunk,' I said.

Tony nodded. 'I thought as much. Tanya is too. She just threw up all over Simon. He's trying to get some water down her. You go and wait for Izzie. I'll sort Nesta out now.'

I nodded and made my way back over to near the stage. I could see that Izzie had been watching with concern whilst trying to carry on at the same time. *I could kill Nesta,* I thought. *She's not only ruined the lovely time I was having with Tony, this is so the last thing that Izzie needed.*

After the gig was finished, I waited backstage for Iz and filled her in on everything.

'Is she OK?' she asked.

'Tony's with her. But never mind her, are you OK? You were brilliant by the way.'

Izzie nodded. 'Yeah, yeah, I'm fine and I guess you have to be prepared for the odd nutter in the audience – just you never expect it to be one of your best mates.'

My mobile beeped with a text to say that mum would be outside at eleven so I went to tell Tony because she was giving Izzie and Nesta a lift too. I ran into him the minute I got outside the hall.

'Have you seen Nesta?' he asked, his face full of anxiety.

'No. I came to ask you that. I thought she was with you.'

'She was. I told her that your mum would be here soon and she went all weird saying that it would make Cressida's night to see you all getting into your mum's jalopy. I told her that it didn't matter what they thought but she went off saying she was going to the loo and now I can't find her anywhere. Honest, Luce, I don't know what's wrong with her lately.'

'I know. Me and Iz have been worried about her too.'

He disappeared back into the hall and then, to my relief, Nesta appeared. 'Sorry, sorry,' she began.

I'd had enough. 'Honestly, Nesta, it was Izzie's big night but you managed to get all the attention as usual.' I looked around to see that Mum's car was pulling up a short distance away. It *was* an old jalopy, Nesta was right. It was an ancient Volkswagen Beetle painted turquoise and I used to be embarrassed about the fact that it stood out like a sore thumb, but lately, it didn't seem to matter any more. Izzie arrived so I linked my arm with hers. I really felt for her. Mum waved and Izzie and I began to walk towards the car. I turned to check that Nesta was behind us but she'd disappeared into the night.

Hell. Now where has she gone? I thought as I told Izzie to tell Mum to wait then went to find Tony.

Tony

'Is there anyone still in there?' I said to a tall blonde girl who was coming out of the Ladies.

She shrugged. 'Dunno,' she said. I pushed past her and into the Ladies. 'Oi,' the girl called back at me. 'It is the *Ladies*. The Gents is over there.'

'I know. I'm looking for my sister,' I said.

'Yeah right,' said the girl, but luckily she didn't hassle me. I checked all cubicles. Empty. Every one. Where the hell was she? Mum and Dad would kill me if I went back without her. I'd managed to persuade Lucy's mum to go, taking Lucy and Izzie, but they didn't look very happy about it although I promised to call them if I had any news and told them that Simon was also looking for her. Lucy had said she didn't know whether to be mad with Nesta or feel sorry for her. She had looked in a total state. Lucy told me what that stuck-up bitch Cressida had said about her. I felt the same way as Lucy, mad with Nesta and sad for her. The idiot.

I went back into the hall. The last people were putting on coats and jackets and leaving. A cleaner arrived and was wearily setting about mopping the floor. The lights were switched on and the whole place was blasted into brightness. It stank of stale beer. No sign of Nesta.

I went back out on to the street.

'I've looked down all the alleys near here and she's not on the street anywhere,' said Simon coming over to me. He looked as worried as I felt. 'Do you think she'll have made her own way home?'

'Don't know,' I said. 'I've tried calling her mobile but she's not picking up. So she's either gone for the bus or tube but I can't imagine Nesta doing either at this time of night. She's got more sense.'

'Except she wasn't her usual self,' said Simon. 'I am so sorry about the booze. I will kill Tanya when I get home.'

'Have they gone?'

Simon nodded. 'I packed her and Cress off in the Mercedes with our driver.'

'You could have gone home too, mate,' I said. 'Nesta's my sister.'

'And my girlfriend.'

We swapped mobile numbers and Simon went one way, I went the other. My stomach was in a knot. Kentish Town on a Friday night was not the place for a girl Nesta's age to be on her own, especially a girl who had had too much to drink and wasn't used to it. I wanted to phone home but didn't want to alarm Mum and Dad in case Nesta *had* got home safe. Knowing her, she'd be tucked up in bed oblivious to the worry she'd caused. But what if she wasn't? Oh where the hell was she? Anything could have happened. I tried to shut off the waves of images that were flooding my mind. Front-page disaster headlines every one. *Nesta, you idiot,* I thought.

A short time later, Simon called. 'No sign. You?'

'Nothing,' I said. 'I've been to the tube and to the bus stop. I think I'm going to go home. I'll call as soon as I know anything.'

'Thanks,' said Simon.

Lucy called too. 'No sign,' I said.

I caught the tube then raced the short distance it was from the station to our flat. I opened the front door and was hit by a horrible smell. Vomit and disinfectant. Dad was on his knees mopping up. He didn't look happy.

'You and I need words,' he said and with a jerk of his head indicated that I should go into the kitchen.

I stepped over the bucket. 'Nesta's back then?'

Dad nodded. 'Ten minutes ago. Threw up all over the hall.'

All I could feel was relief as I pulled out my mobile to let Simon, Lucy and Izzie know.

Lucy

Lucy's diary
20th April

Boys snogged: 2

I think I may be in love with Tony again. We had a major snog sesh the night of Izzie's gig and it reminded me just how great a kisser he is. I have one boy to compare him to now and that's Eddie Mason. It happened last Wednesday night in the car park behind the cinema in Muswell Hill. I was waiting for Dad and Eddie was there carrying a load of shopping for his mum who went off to get more groceries. I've known him for ages and although I don't really fancy him, I knew he fancied me – he's always been after me at parties – so I decided to give it a go. I wanted to kiss another boy besides Tony, just to see what it was like. It was yuk. We were all out of synch with each other and his lips were too wet. Not at all like with Tone.

The way he handled the whole mad Nesta night really impressed me. He was so protective of her. Izzie and I let her stew for a few days after the gig but we missed her too much so when she came round grovelling, it didn't take long before we had all agreed to be best of mates for ever and ever again. Simon's sister Tanya had taken a bottle of champagne to the gig and Nesta had swigged it back like it was lemonade. I think she also wanted to prove to Tanya how grown up and sophisticated she could be. Tony told me that she had a bad hangover and was so miserable afterwards. She tried to finish with Simon saying that she couldn't keep up with his crowd, but he wasn't having any of it and that he didn't see it as his crowd or her crowd. He's cool. Not at all stuck up like Cressida.

Not sure what to do about Tony though cos Nesta said he had a girlfriend a week or so ago but he wasn't with her at the gig and he certainly didn't act like someone who was in a relationship when we snogged on the dance floor. I have to think about how to play it because I know he likes a challenge so I don't want to go diving in there and blow it. I shall watch and wait from a distance. And maybe do a few Izzie spells. Tee hee. She says I have to get a photo of him, sprinkle it with sugar, put it in an envelope under my pillow and he will grow sweet on me. That's if mice don't eat it.

Noticed that a girl called TJ Watts in our class looks lonely. She was mates with a girl called Hannah who left to go and live in South Africa. Must put it to the others that we should ask her to hang out with us for a bit. She's cool and I've always liked her. She's dead brainy.

Tony

Splash of the old Armani and away we go. Tonight's a very special night. May the twenty-fourth and I'm taking Lucy out for her birthday. I've saved up my pocket money for a few weeks plus Dad bunged me a bit extra. It's going to be a romantic meal in an Italian restaurant on the Archway Road then a walk in the park. It's a lovely evening so we may just let nature take its course.

She was waiting for me outside Jackson's Lane opposite Highgate tube. It was funny because both of our faces lit up when we saw each other and both of us tried to hide it and to look cool. We laughed because we knew exactly what we were doing. It's like that with Lucy – as if she can read my mind almost. She looked great, in blue – it really suits her. She has some style, does Lucy, clothes look good on her. It bothers her that she's small. Not even five foot I think, but I like being taller than her. Makes me feel protective.

We held hands as we walked towards the restaurant and it

felt totally natural even though we weren't going out officially. This was our first proper date since Izzie's gig. We'd been chatting on the phone about what a total eejit my sister had been – so juvenile – and then called each other a couple of times after that. In one chat, Lucy had mentioned that it was her birthday this week so I jumped in and asked her out. I was surprised that she said yes because she'd been cool with me after Izzie's gig, like she'd lost interest, which was strange after our steamy snog on the dance floor. I guess that was part of the challenge with her though. She wasn't a pushover for my charm and that only made me want to win her over more.

The restaurant was perfect. Not too posy, not too down-market, just comfortable. The waiter made a big fuss of Lucy when he found out that it was her birthday and she blushed like anything when he came out with all the waiters with tambourines and sang 'Happy Birthday' to her. We both stuffed our faces. My dad's Italian and I love good Italian food. We both had pasta. I noticed that we'd both picked dishes with no garlic. Snogging was deffo on the cards. We devoured huge bowls of tiramisu afterwards. On the house, the manager said. I think he was smitten with Lucy too. One thing I like about her is that she likes her food. I've been on some dates with girls who are so picky and go on about being on a diet and the size of their bums or legs. What they don't realise is that boys love those curvy bits.

After supper, we headed over towards Highgate Woods where we found a bench tucked away from the main paths. I noticed that Lucy had gone quiet on me.

'You OK?' I said.

She nodded and rubbed her tummy. 'Yeah. Full to burst.'

'Me too,' I said and I put my arm around her.

We started to kiss and as always with her, it felt great, *really great* and after a while I couldn't stop myself – part of me just wanted to eat her up – I caressed her shoulders, the back of her neck, her arms, round to the front . . .

She smacked my hands away and leaped up. 'Tony! I told you before.'

'I . . . I'm sorry. I get carried away. Sorry. Sit down. I won't do again. Promise.'

She sat down again and I started to tickle her instead. She laughed and began to tickle me back and soon we were wrestling. A man with his dog went by and looked across at us suspiciously.

'You all right, love?' he asked Lucy.

She nodded and pointed at me. 'He's got ants in his pants.'

The man rolled his eyes, huffed and walked off. I tried to catch her to tickle her again, but she ran off. I soon caught her up and wrestled her to the ground. I sat on top of her and pinned her arms down with my knees and then I leaned in. 'OK, no escaping this time.' And we had a really long snog. I changed position and lay beside her but cuddled her into me. It felt great lying there in the grass on a warm spring night, the stars up above, really romantic. I began to edge on top of her and pulled her closer to me, but she pushed me off. She got up, brushed the grass off her skirt and then she just looked at me.

I stuck my tongue out. 'Meanie.'

She didn't laugh or even smile. 'I want to go home now.'

She began to walk towards the park gate. I scrambled to my feet to go with her. I would never leave a girl to go home on her own. That's not my style, even if we'd just had an argument, which I think we'd just had . . . Sort of. Sometimes I don't get what's going on in girls' minds. I thought she was well into it. Into me. By the expression on her face and the determined way that she was walking away from me, clearly not. What did I do wrong?

Lucy

'You OK?' asked Izzie as we got changed into our sleepover gear. Izzie, TJ and I were staying over at Nesta's for the night and she had gone for supplies with TJ, leaving me alone with Iz.

I shrugged. 'Ish. I just don't want to bump into Tony. Remember last time we had a sleepover here? I ended up in his room and things got a bit hot and then again in the park when we went out for my birthday.'

'Don't worry,' said Izzie. 'I know for a fact that he's staying with a mate over in Hampstead. Apparently when he heard that we were all coming over, he immediately said he was going out.'

'How do you know?'

'Nesta told me.'

I was about to ask her if she had told Nesta about Tony getting fresh with me. I hadn't told Nesta myself. Not that I didn't trust her. I did, but she was still Tony's sister and I didn't want to make trouble between the two of them. I got the feeling that if she knew how much he had been coming on to me, she might kill him. I could talk to Izzie about it though.

'I'm just not ready to go further than kissing with Tony but I also feel embarrassed about my total lack in the boob area. You know I have the chest of a nine-year-old girl.'

'I doubt that would put him off,' said Izzie. 'He clearly adores you.'

'He adores me when he can't have me. It's the challenge he adores.'

Izzie shrugged. 'Maybe —'

At that moment, TJ and Nesta came in so we quickly changed the subject. They had brought a tray laden down with all our fave sleepover goodies: crisps, choc-chip cookies, slices of pizza and Liquorice Allsorts. TJ was such a sweetie, a little shy at first but now I was getting to know her, I was glad we'd asked her to join our gang. She was a good laugh and I think she'll make a good fourth mate.

We had a great night doing our usual sleepover activities: we watched a couple of romantic movies from Nesta's dad's classic collection. He has some brillopad ones. This time we watched *The Philadelphia Story* which was made in the nineteen-fifties and then we watched *Sleepless in Seattle* which made all of us cry when the hero (Tom Hanks) and the heroine (Meg Ryan) get together at the end. We ate everything naughty including all the cookies and then Nesta insisted that we danced off all the calories we had eaten so we went round the world and did our version of Scottish, Egyptian, Hawaiian, African, Irish, Indian and Aborigine dancing. It was hysterical and TJ joined in with gusto like she'd been doing mad dancing her whole life. I was very relieved that Tony wasn't around because I wouldn't have wanted him to catch me in my jim-jams dancing like a loonie petunie.

'I love sleepovers with you guys,' I said when we collapsed in a heap on the sofa. 'These are the best times in the world and make me wonder why I even bother with boys. Boys just mess your head and your heart up. Girls help sort your head out and heal your heart.'

'Yay,' said Izzie.

'Er, I wouldn't rule boys out,' said Nesta. 'They have their uses.'

I couldn't totally disagree because secretly a part of me was hoping that Tony might come back later and we'd have a chance to do some flirting.

TJ was so funny when we got on to talking about boys. She reckons she's very inexperienced. 'See, I can karate chop a boy to the floor and stand on his neck easy peasy, but if I think of having to kiss one, I'm terrified,' she confessed. She's a whizz at sports and is a champion arm wrestler, but she said it's when it comes to boys that she loses confidence. 'I turn into Noola the alien girl and I talk gibberish.' I wasn't sure whether to tell her or not but my brother Steve is totally into her. He's been asking about her since she first came round to our house. I could tell he was well impressed – the way she mended his computer and knew all about the books he was into. I could see his mind ticking over: *A babe? With a brain? Could this be possible?* I decided to wait before I told her because although TJ's a new mate, Steve is my brother and I wasn't sure that he'd want me blurting out his secret crush. It was up to him to tell her that he was into her, not me. I'd definitely want Tony to tell me his feelings before Nesta, even if she is his sister.

'We'll look after you,' said Nesta. 'Stick with us and we'll teach you everything we know about boys.'

'Which isn't a lot,' said Izzie.

Nesta grinned. 'Speak for yourself.'

The next morning, Nesta's mum and dad made themselves scarce and went out to Highgate village to have their breakfast up there so we took over the kitchen. We'd got up late and we were still in our pyjamas sitting around eating toast when Tony arrived back around eleven. I took a deep breath and tried to look uninterested although that was the total opposite of what I was feeling. I always reacted when I saw Tony; either my stomach flipped or my knees went to jelly. Not that I was ever going to let on to him though. He'd love it. Nesta went straight into introductions between him and TJ and we got to witness first hand how she turned into her alien girl. She blushed furiously (*Hurrah, another blusher,* I thought) as Tony turned on the charm and gave her a flirty look. 'Hi, TJ,' he said in a low voice.

TJ looked at him then at the floor. 'Uhuh,' she muttered.

'So TJ, what do virgins eat for breakfast?' he asked.

TJ blushed even more. 'Um . . . dunno,' she replied.

'Thought not,' he said with a grin.

'Take no notice of Tony, he's a dingbat,' said Nesta.

Poor TJ, I thought and I gave Tony a look as if to say, 'Lay off her.' He grinned back at me. I wondered if he was grinning at me because I looked a mess. I had thought about dashing to the loo to make sure that my hair wasn't sticking up all over the place but I couldn't put any make-up on or lip-gloss because it would look too obvious and strange with my night clothes. *Oh well, tough,* I thought. *If he doesn't like me as I am,* au naturel, *then he doesn't like the real me.* I stuck my tongue out at him which made him grin even more. He went to the fridge and got out a half-eaten apple pie. He cut himself a huge slice.

'Apple pie for breakfast, gross,' said Izzie.

'Would you prefer I did something else with it?' he asked with a cheeky expression on his face.

'Like what?' asked Izzie.

'You seen that film *American Pie*?'

'Yeah,' said Izzie, then she pulled a face. 'Eww and double eww.'

TJ looked mystified.

Nesta sighed. 'Sorry about my disgusting brother, TJ. In *American Pie*, a boy asks what it's like to have sex. His mate says it's like putting your thingee in a warm apple pie.'

Tony watched TJ to see her reaction. She blushed even more. I decided that I'd give him a taste of his own medicine and take the focus off TJ. I slipped off my stool. 'Apparently, some guy in Australia tried it, but this guy didn't wait for the pie to cool after it came out of the oven. He was taken to the local hospital and treated for burns.'

Tony's hands flew to his crotch. 'Arghhhh!' he said as the rest of us cracked up laughing. 'I wonder how he explained *that* to the nurse on duty.'

I picked up the apple pie. 'Er, Tony . . . would you like me to warm that up for you? I could put it in the microwave . . . on high.'

Tony laughed, came over and put his arm around me. 'And how is the love of my life?'

I wriggled away from him. 'Dunno. How is she?'

'You know you want me really,' he said.

'Yeah right. It's *agony* keeping my hands off you. Not,' I said and headed for the door with the others.

Tony sighed. 'That girl . . . ' I heard him say as we made our exit.

It was hard resisting him when he came close and I felt the vibe between us, but it was also fun keeping him on his toes.

Tony

'Blimey, it's a bit posh here,' said Rob when we got to the party on Saturday night. It was in Knightsbridge. A mega posh place. Huge rooms, marble floors, with a smell of . . . ? Money. A doorman in black tie let us in and once inside, his clone stepped forward and offered something pink and bubbly in a champagne flute glass.

'Just act like you own the place, like you totally belong,' I said to Rob after I'd taken a flute, then I looked around for Annabelle. I'd met her last year at a party in Holland Park. Luckily I didn't have far to look. She was coming out of a room to our left into the hall and waved when she saw me. I felt relieved because I could see the doorman glancing down at his list then back at us. He was about to say something to Rob but backed off when he saw that Annabelle knew us.

'Hey Annabelle,' I said as I made my way over.

She flicked her long blond hair back and turned to a boy

behind her. 'Hey Tony, meet my new boyfriend, Sebastian Janson Hicks.'

A smooth-looking boy of about eighteen stepped forward. I nodded at him. 'Great party,' I said.

He looked down his long nose at me. 'How do you know? You just arrived.'

Annabelle giggled nervously. 'Take no notice of Seb.'

Tosser, I thought as scanned the room. 'First impressions, mate, first impressions count and it doesn't hurt to make guests welcome.'

Sebastian looked momentarily confused. I thought about leaving. I didn't really know people here and I wasn't going to stay if the rest of Annabelle's guests were like him.

And then I saw her.

Slim with long, white-blond hair, face of an angel, body of a goddess. She was all in black and wearing one of those low-cut corset things. Sexy. She clocked me too. I held her gaze a moment, a moment longer then I turned my back on her. She'd find me later if she'd felt it.

'Come on, Rob, let's find some nosh. I'm starving,' I said and pulled him away towards the kitchen.

We didn't find the nosh. The nosh found us. A fleet of men in black-and-white were taking around plates of tasty morsels: shepherd's pies, chicken pieces on sticks, pizza pieces, beef and noodles, all *à la* miniature. Rob and I positioned ourselves by the kitchen door and grabbed them all. We were starving. I hadn't had a thing since breakfast with Nesta and her mates. It had been nice to see Lucy, always is, but she's playing it very cool these days. *Time to move on,* I told myself. *Find someone more my own age or . . . let her find me,* I thought as I watched the girl with the white-blond hair come out into the hall as if she was looking for someone.

Nigellas, Savannahs, Jeremys, Simons, Mariellas, came and went. Rob and I munched on whatever was doing the rounds and I waited until angel face made her move. I didn't have to wait long. Just as the bowtie boys were bringing in the mini puddings, she wafted my way in a breeze of perfume. *Lovely,* I thought. *I like a girl who smells nice.*

'So how do you know Annabelle?' she asked casually, looking around as she asked.

'I'm her personal trainer,' I said and then indicated Rob. 'And this is her shrink, Rob. Needless to say Rob sees more of her than I do.'

She laughed a tinkly laugh. Nice. I don't like girls who hee haw.

'And you?' I asked.

'I am her divorce lawyer,' she replied. 'OK, she's only young but she'll need me in the future.'

Good reply, I thought. I laughed and Rob read the signs, good man, and made himself scarce.

By the end of the evening, she was mine. Nicky. A date, next week and, if it went well, I'd take her to Aiden's party and show her how we partied up in North London.

Lucy

Lucy's diary

5th June

Dear diary, I am sorry I neglect you, it must be hard being a diary. Some weeks you get a lot of attention, some weeks you get none. Well, I can sympathise. I really can. Tony has been neglecting me like I have been neglecting you and it hurts. We're supposed to be playing a game, cat and mouse type thing, but it feels like I am playing solo lately. Cue the song, *All by myse-e-elf,* to be sung in a diva voice. Yep. I have been busy being aloof and a challenge waiting for Tony to win me back but it feels like he's lost interest.

Maybe time to change my game and let him know that I'm not as disinterested as I seem. And, dear diary, I will try not to neglect you so much either.

15th June

Hi diary. Tony still not around much and every time I've been over to Nesta's, he's been out. Convenient, I think. Exam time, says

Nesta. He's been staying behind at the school library a lot. Hmm. Have been v. tempted to give in and call him, but resisted. He's not the kind of boy who likes to be chased and also he might need his space to do exams. I know he takes schoolwork seriously. Roll on summer, that's all I can say.

'This has to be the best feeling in the world,' I said to Nesta as we got out of the school gates.

'I know,' she said. 'Summer hols. Six weeks with no Miss Watkins . . . Six fabola weeks with Simon before he goes off to uni.'

'And six weeks with Ben for me,' said Izzie.

'And I suppose we'll be seeing you around at ours a fair bit,' I said to TJ. She's been seeing my elder brother Steve over the last few weeks.

'What about you, Lucy?' asked Nesta. 'Going to give *my* poor brother a break? You've been giving him the run around for months now. I don't think his ego can stand much more of it.'

I grinned and pulled an envelope out of my rucksack. 'I haven't really been giving him the run around, you know I haven't. Just haven't seen him. I've been doing some thinking about him lately though and I've come to a decision.'

'Which is?'

'I've written him a card saying no more messing about, that I really like him and would like to get together over the summer.'

The girls made various encouraging sounds so my plan was clearly OK by them. I'd been the odd one out lately, being the only singleton amongst us, and I felt that it was time to change that. I was ready for a 'proper' relationship and I could no longer come up with any reason why Tony and I shouldn't go forward. I liked him, he liked me. Being cool all the time and not knowing what was really going on was getting boring when there could be some serious snog sessions happening instead. If he tried it on, I'd just be firm. My plan was to post the note and he'd get it first thing in the morning, so the first post box that we saw as we made our way down the road, I popped it in.

Six glorious weeks to hang out with Tony. We'd all have a boyfriend. It could be the summer to remember!

The phone in the hall rang soon after I'd got home.

'For you,' Mum called to me.

I went into the hall and picked up the receiver. It was Tony.

'Hi,' he said. 'What are you doing later? Fancy meeting up? I, er, want to talk to you about something.'

Ohmigod, I thought. He wants to see me. Wants to talk to me. This is so amazing. I just know he's going to ask me if we can date seriously. It has to be that. The last few times I've seen him, he has hinted at it. We are so in tune.

He asked me to meet him in Raj's café in Highgate so after I'd put down the phone, I changed into my jeans and a clean T-shirt. A squirt of perfume and a slick of lip-gloss and I was off.

As I sat on the bus, I decided not to say anything about the card. It would be so sweet. He'd ask me about hanging out in the summer and I can play it cool just a bit longer and say I have to think about it and then tomorrow, he'll get my card and know that we'd been thinking along exactly the same lines all the time. It would be so romantic. It was working out so perfectly.

Tony

Rob walked up the hill towards Raj's café with me.

'It will be OK. Lucy's cool,' I said.

Rob looked at me with disbelief. 'You're going to tell her that you've met someone else. Yeah. Sure. It will be OK.'

'Well maybe not that I've met someone else, I just want to get things clear with her so she doesn't get hurt.'

'As in, "Can we be friends?"' said Rob. 'Yeah. I think everyone knows exactly what that means.'

'I do want to be friends with her. I do, but no way would I ever come out with that line to her. I know I've used it before but she deserves better. I am *not* looking forward to this.'

'No. Wouldn't imagine you are, mate. Think I'd rather chew my own arm off, in fact,' said Rob.

'Yeah, be easier. I don't know. What am I going to say? How do I put it?'

'Lucy, you're dumped?' Rob offered.

'But she isn't dumped. That's just it. We aren't even going out properly. I haven't even seen her around lately. We've kept missing each other – when she's been over to see Nesta, I've been somewhere else.'

'So why do you feel the need to do this? You don't owe her anything.'

'I know. I . . . She . . . I don't want to hurt her.'

'And you think when you tell her that you're dating a top babe, you think that's not going to hurt her?'

I shrugged. 'I don't know. I . . . I promised my sister that I wouldn't mess Lucy around and I don't want her finding out about Nicky from anyone else.'

'If you like Lucy so much – and it's clear that you do – why don't you just go for it with her? Date her.'

'Because she's young. She's only fourteen. And . . . '

Rob gave me a knowing look. 'She won't put out and Nicky will.'

'Nicky's older. And OK, yeah – Lucy doesn't want the serious stuff and I don't want to push her. Too close to home with my sis being one of her best mates. It could get complicated.'

'More complicated than it is already?' Rob scoffed.

'Yeah,' I said. We'd reached the doorway to Raj's café.

Rob put his hand on my shoulder. 'Good luck, soldier. It was nice knowing you.'

'Yeah, thanks,' I said.

I had such mixed feelings about meeting Lucy. I couldn't deny that part of me was looking forward to seeing her but another part was dreading it because the last thing I wanted to do was upset her, but I knew that it couldn't happen between us. Like I'd said to Rob, I'd realised she was too young for me.

Rob went off down the road and I opened the door to the café, took a deep breath and went upstairs to where we'd agreed to meet. Lucy hadn't arrived yet so I took a table in the corner away from the other people in there having tea.

I like Raj's. It's a funky place with old furniture that looks like it belongs in a church – pews instead of seats – and the man who owns it has loads of interesting old books and other stuff about the place.

I didn't have to wait long. I heard the door ping downstairs and I felt a rush of anxiety. I knew it was her and there she was a few moments later, slightly breathless from the stairs, blushing as she always did when she saw me. This was going to be really hard. She slid in behind the table and I ordered her a Coke and we chatted generally for a bit, about school, about what I was reading, about the strange stuff around the café: Russian dolls, old sepia photos, strange bits of old china.

'So you had something you wanted to say?' Lucy finally asked.

'Um, yeah,' I said, then I tried to buy myself some more time by asking about what she was up to over the holidays.

She looked into my eyes, straight into them, and said in a suggestive way, 'No definite plans. Got any ideas?'

She was coming on to me. She was. Least I think she was. Was this really the best time to tell her about Nicky? 'Not really,' I stuttered. 'That is, Lucy . . . How can I put this?'

She was looking at me in a really weird way, like half smiling, teasing almost, leaning forward, her hand resting next to mine on the table. Had Nesta told her about Nicky? She couldn't have. I had purposely not filled her in this time although we normally talk about who we're dating. This time I wanted to tell Lucy first. I took a deep breath. 'Thing is, Luce, well, we've been on and off for ages now and I wanted to get things straight between us. It's not fair on you and it's not fair on me. We've got the holidays ahead of us and it's like a new chapter for both of us, so . . . so, what I think is that, er . . . maybe we should make a clean slate of it.'

Lucy's face clouded and she leaned back and crossed her arms. 'Clean slate? What are you saying?'

'Well it's not like we're boyfriend and girlfriend, are we? We never really have been.'

She looked hurt. Oh God. *Really* hurt. She was trying to cover it and gave me a sort of fake grin, like a kid who's fallen over and is trying to be brave. 'No. No. Course not.'

'And I was thinking that, what if, say, you meet someone this holiday or I meet someone? It's kind of confusing. Our situation, that is . . . me and you. Well, we're not free and we're not really committed.'

Lucy's expression had hardened. 'No, we're not.'

'So what do you think?'

'I'm not sure I understand. Are you saying that you want to be committed or that you want to meet someone else?'

Oh God, think Tony, I told myself. *This is really important. You have to say it right. God I hate this. This is exactly why I don't want to get to committed to one girl. You only end up hurting them.* 'That I want to be free,' I blurted.

'You're dumping me?' asked Lucy. She had such a wounded

expression in her eyes. I felt like a monster.

'No, no. Course not. How can I dump you when we were never going out properly?'

'But . . . ' she started.

I reached for her hand, but she snatched it away. *This sucks,* I thought, *and it's not my fault. I am trying to do the decent thing here.* I felt *so* frustrated.

'Look, Lucy, it's not as though I haven't asked you out in the past but you always put me off.'

'I didn't know how I felt then,' she said. 'It wasn't that I was putting you off, but . . . '

This wasn't going well, I needed to reassure her. 'I'm not dumping you. I'm getting it straight, so we both know where we are. We can still be friends.' *D'oh! Arghhh! I'd said it!*

Lucy took a sharp intake of breath as if I'd hit her. She knew what that old 'let's be friends' line meant too. She looked as if she was going to cry.

She got up. 'Got to go,' she blurted and headed for the door.

'But what about your Coke?' I called after her as the waiter came over with her drink.

'You have it,' she called over her shoulder.

Well, that went well – not, I thought as I let my forehead sink forward to rest on the table.

Lucy

Once I got outside Raj's, I looked in my bag for my mobile. Stupid tears kept getting in the way. Couldn't see it. Darn it. It was still in my rucksack at home. I had to get hold of Nesta. I *had* to get her tomorrow morning to catch the post before Tony got to it and saw my card. *Oh hell, I wish I'd never sent it,* I thought as I raced home with tears stinging my eyes. *I will never commit anything like that to paper again. I am an idiot, idiot, idiot.* Total embarrassment on top of my heart being torn apart would be more than I could take. *This* is why people play it cool. You choose someone wholeheartedly and then your heart gets ripped to shreds.

I opened the door and legged it through the hall. Mum Dad, Steve and Lal were eating.

'Lucy,' Mum called.

'Later,' I shouted as I grabbed my rucksack, headed up the stairs, pulled out my phone and rang Nesta. *Argh!* Her mobile was off. I tried the landline. She wasn't at home either. I left a message on Nesta's voicemail. Then I texted her. Then I emailed. *I can't breathe,* I thought as I lay on the bed and groaned as panic rose from my stomach into my chest. *It's all been in my head, my stupid head,* I thought. *He doesn't care about me at all. Never has. It really has all just been a game to him. He's never been into me the way I'm into him. I really thought we had something special and if he gets that card I am going to be exposed for the naive idiot that I am.*

Hah! Only hours ago I had been saying it was the best day ever, school was out. Now it was the worst day ever and it wasn't even over yet.

Tony

Got up early to go and play five-a-side footie down in Hyde Park. Nicky is coming later to cheer me on. As I trudged towards the kitchen to grab a cup of coffee, the morning post plopped through the letterbox and on to the mat.

I bent to pick the letters up. One for me. That's unusual. Girlie handwriting. *It's not Valentine's or my birthday,* I thought. I took the envelope and went into the kitchen, made myself a cup of coffee then opened my post.

It was from Lucy. A sort of poem.

I'm not changing,

I'm just rearranging,

my life to be with you.

Then she'd written: *Sorry for messing you about over the last year, but now I'm ready. I know we have something really special and I want to make a go of it. Call me.*

Holy shitola, I thought as I glanced at the postmark. She must have posted this yesterday before we met up.

Talk about bad timing, I thought as I reached for the phone to call her. I put it down again. What could I possibly say?

Lucy

Lucy's diary

30th July

My life is over. My reputation as a coolster ruined for ever. My humiliation on this planet of sorrow and heartbreak is now complete. Not only have I been dumped by Tony, dumped when we weren't even going out (how sad is that?), but after racing from the café and leaving a million messages for Nesta which she didn't get, apparently Tony opened the card that I'd sent him in the post.

He's called a few times but I wouldn't speak to him. I don't want to speak to anyone for a while. I want to climb into a hole and only come out when I'm seventy-five and probably not even then. Dad's trying to drag me off to a New Age retreat in Cornwall for a few days but he doesn't understand that I have retreated from LIFE, no New Age hocus pocus can help me. I am beyond saving. Sadly my mates weren't having any of this and organised a 'Let's Find Lucy a Boy' campaign. DISASTER. There just aren't any boys that even compare to Tony. He has ruined me for all others. And the WORST thing is we went to a party at the weeekend and Tony turned up with a girl, a totally gorgeous blonde girl who looked sophisticated and experienced in the naughty department and was Wonderbra-ed up to her neck!

Izzie said I had to face my fears, to not leave things unfinished and that I should talk to him. Instead I came home and finished a tub of Ben and Jerry's, a packet of Rolos and a packet of double chocolate chip cookies. Somehow I don't think that those were the sorts of unfinished things she had in mind. Tough.

Tony

'Have you heard from Lucy?' I asked Nesta.

Nesta slathered sun cream on her arms. 'Might have. What is it to you?' she asked. It was a few weeks after the Lucy incident and it was a glorious day, not a cloud in the sky and we were out on our back patio making the most of it.

'Oh come on, Nesta, give me a break, I was trying to do the right thing,' I said as I turned over on my sun lounger to give my back some rays.

'Well, I *have* got some news. Izzie called this morning from Cornwall. *Very interesting* news, actually.'

'What?' I asked. It *really* annoyed me having to go through my sister like this, especially when she loves to lord it when she has a secret or a juicy titbit that she knows I'd like to know.

Nesta tapped the side of her nose. 'For me to know and you to find out,' she said.

I knew she wouldn't be able to keep it in for too long though because Nesta has a big mouth and can't keep a secret once she's made the point that she knows something that I don't.

'What? She's become a Buddhist? Drowned in the sea? Eaten too many Cornish cream teas and become a porker?'

Lucy and Izzie had taken off with Lucy's dad and Izzie's mum on a New Age retreat, that much I did know because Nesta was forever texting them down there. Plus I'd bumped into TJ in Highgate Wood when she was walking the Loverings' dogs and her dog with Lucy's brother, Steve. TJ had also mentioned that Lucy had gone.

'No, nothing like that,' said Nesta. 'She's met someone.'

'Someone? You mean a boy?'

Nesta nodded. 'And he's supposed to be totally gorgeous. His name is Daniel and he's a blond god with a six pack to die for and he's a fashion student like Lucy is and Izzie said that it's like they were made for each other and they have loads in common and she hasn't seen Lucy so happy for —'

'OK, you can shut up now,' I said. I was jealous, no doubt about it. A stab deep in the pit of my stomach. Mad really because things were going well with Nicky. She was a babe to be seen with. She brought out envy factor ten whenever anyone from school saw us together. I reckon we'd last the summer at least.

'But I thought you wanted to know how Lucy is,' gloated Nesta.

I got the sun lotion bottle, took off the top and squirted it at her. It landed with a satisfying splat all over her forehead. Result!

'Toneeeeee,' Nesta groaned.

Unfortunately it was at the exact moment that Mum came out of the French doors.

'Tony! For heaven's sake, when are you going to grow up?!' she demanded.

Nesta gave me a smug look. 'He's just jealous because Lucy has a fab new boyfriend.'

Sometimes I hate my sister.

Lucy

'Have you introduced Daniel to Izzie, TJ and Nesta yet?' asked Mum as she served up supper – spag bol with soya mince.

'Tomorrow,' I said. 'TJ's busy but Nesta and Izzie are coming to Notting Hill Gate with us.'

Lal wrapped his arms round himself and made loud slurpy noises which I think were supposed to represent kissing. I ignored him. I have found that the best method to deal with most juvenile boys is to take no notice of their stupidity. That and a good thump to the solar plexus every now and again.

I'd had the most amazing time with Daniel since I'd met him in Cornwall. Best of all, it had turned out that he didn't live far from us in London so we had been able to meet up loads. In the last few weeks, we had done London as tourists and, seeing as both of us are into fashion and design, we'd done art galleries and exhibitions and some posh clothes shops. He seemed to know about so many things and I was learning so much from him.

I could have introduced him to my mates but I hadn't wanted to share him at first. It was only in the last week I had been missing my friends – but it was hard to make plans to see Izzie, TJ or Nesta because Daniel always had an itinerary for us. He was so sweet, sending me text messages saying what we could do the next day, five minutes after he'd left me. And he'd bought me a little teddy bear because he said it reminded him of me. He was so romantic and was the perfect remedy to help me get over Tony. In fact, I'd hardly thought about him at all.

Tony

I was watching a DVD on Saturday evening when Nesta came in to the living room, threw down her bag then flung herself back on to the sofa.

'Where have you been?' I asked.

'Notting Hill,' she snapped.

'Wow, you're in a strop.'

She crossed her arms and glowered. 'So would you be.'

'Why? Been dumped by Simon?'

'No. As if,' she said then she looked up at me. 'I don't know if I should tell you this . . .'

'Don't then,' I said. I knew she would. I could see a mile off that she was bursting to unload something.

'OK, but you must never *ever* tell Lucy I told you.'

Lucy. I paused the movie. 'Cross my heart, your secret is safe with me.'

Nesta sat up. 'She is going out with this total loser.'

'Loser?' I tried to keep the enthusiasm out of my voice. 'I

thought he was supposed to be God's gift.'

'OK, not loser – granted, he is very good-looking, but boy, doesn't he know it? I lost count of the number of times I caught him checking his reflection in a shop window.'

'Really?' Inwardly I punched the air. I hadn't liked the idea of Lucy dating Mr Perfect Pants. What Nesta was saying was music to my ears.

'Yeah and he was all over her in a really creepy way – but the sad thing is that Lucy can't even see it. He's so full of himself, like when we met, we asked him about himself but *he* didn't ask one thing – not one question back about us.'

I laughed. 'Yeah I can see that would be very annoying for you, sis.'

'Shut it. He lectured us all afternoon about what he knew about fashion and you know what? Lucy let him. She knew all that stuff he was telling us but she kept shtoom like it was new to her. She was acting like a total doormat pathetic drip and that's not Luce. For example, he ordered for her in a café. He ordered an espresso for her.'

'But she hates strong coffee.'

'Exactly. And he had his arm round her the whole time and was kissing her and holding her hand. Honestly, Tone, it was well nauseating.'

'Not feeling jealous are you, by any chance?'

'*No* way. Ask Izzie, she thought he was yuk too. Izzie also said that a mate of Ben's is going out with one of Daniel's exes and apparently she said that Daniel could be difficult, like he was sweet in the beginning and then possessive and clingy in the end, telling her what to do, what to wear, who she could and couldn't see. I think Lucy may be dating a potential psychopathic stalker.'

'I think if she's dating him willingly then he can't be a stalker,' I commented.

'You know what I mean. He's taking her over. Today was the first time in weeks that we have seen her. She has totally neglected her girlfriends for this arrogant plonker.'

'Er . . . don't hold back, Nesta.'

'I won't. I don't like him. She's gone into a couple bubble with him and it's not as if the rest of us don't have boyfriends, we do, but we still know that mates come first every time.'

'Ah, so that's what it's about. You're missing your mate.'

'Yeah, course, but I don't like him either and I don't think he's good for Lucy.'

'That's a shame,' I said then clicked the movie back on like I was totally bored. In my head though, a choir was singing the hallelujah chorus.

I met the man himself a few days later. I'd nipped into Hampstead to find a card for Mum's birthday and there was Lucy on the opposite side of the road. It was the first time I had seen her all through the holidays because the girls hadn't been over for one of their sleepovers lately. Nesta said that they liked to hang out at Izzie's in the summer because her mum and stepfather were always at work so they had the run of the place, plus Mrs Foster's house had the biggest garden. Anyway, there she was in a white T-shirt and shorts, cute as ever.

'Hey Lucy,' I called, then wondered if she was still mad with me and might blank me, but no, she waved so I crossed the road.

'Hi, how are you?' she asked.

'Good. Are you speaking to me then?'

'Yeah, course.'

'I tried ringing you . . . '

'I know. Um, sorry . . . '

She looked great, a bit of tan which made her blue eyes stand out and her hair was bleached lighter than usual from the sun. So cute.

'So what you doing?' I asked.

She held up a Ryman's bag. 'Not much. Just picked these up then I was going to have a wander around the shops.

'Let's go and get a drink and catch up, then,' I said and I linked her arm through mine. 'I haven't seen you in ages.'

We walked down to the Coffee Cup and got a table outside on the pavement. I ordered a Coke. 'What would you like?' I asked.

'Blackcurrant,' she said, pulling a face as a waitress went by with a tiny coffee cup. 'Definitely not espresso.'

I didn't let on that I knew why she'd said that. 'No. Way too bitter, I think.'

'Me too.'

'You're looking good.'

'So are you. Been out in the sun?'

I nodded. 'So, Nesta tells me that you have a new boyfriend.'

'Sort of. And you're still with your girlfriend?'

'Sort of. Actually, no. That's over. Um, she doesn't know yet, though. I don't know how to tell her but . . . nah, it's not working.'

'Why?'

'You know me, I'm not really into having the big relationship. You know, the world of coupledom. And she, well, she's getting a bit heavy, if you know what I mean. Always wanting to see me, like every day, and always phoning wanting to know what I'm doing.'

Lucy nodded like she knew exactly what I meant. 'Too clingy?'

'*Yeah*, I feel like she's taking over my life.'

'Yeah,' Lucy said.

'So how's it going with what's-his-name?' I said, even though I knew exactly what his name was.

'Daniel. Not sure . . . I mean, it was great in the beginning – brilliant, but . . . I don't know. Same thing really. He wants to do the couple bubble thing, just us in there. I don't know if I like it all the time.'

'We got on though, didn't we?' I asked.

She smiled back at me and I felt a rush of chemistry. 'We did. And I'm sorry I over-reacted when you . . . you know, that time in Highgate. I hope we can be mates.'

I put my hand over hers. 'You bet. Always. We get on, we always have. I tell you what, we'll be lovers who used to go out and now we're best of friends.' I knew I was still coming out with the 'let's be friends' line but so was she and I felt we both really meant it. It wasn't a fob off.

'Yeah, best of friends,' she replied, smiling warmly at me.

'Who fancy each other a bit.' I knew I was flirting but there was no denying the chemistry was still there.

She laughed and rolled her eyes. 'Yeah. A bit.'

I laughed too. She was so easy to be with. Fun. Not like Nicky who was *so* intense and lately coming out with those four words that terrify all boys: we need to talk.

'So, this new bloke is clingy, is he?' I asked. Across the road, I was aware of a tall blond boy who had done a double take when he saw Lucy and I sitting together.

'Yeah. Always wanting to know what I'm doing, where I'm going. I feel like he's always checking up on me.'

'Like that boy over there,' I said and nodded at blond boy. 'He's staring at you. You've got an admirer.'

Lucy glanced over then stiffened. She waved and beckoned whoever it was over. He darted through the traffic and came to stand awkwardly besides us.

'Tony, this is Daniel,' said Lucy. 'Daniel, Tony.'

Ah, so this is Mr Perfect Pants. I had to admit he was reasonably good-looking, but he looked so serious. Not fun by anyone's standards. I gave him a half-smile. 'Sit down, join us.'

Daniel shifted about on his feet but he seemed reluctant to sit. *Oops,* I thought. *Time to make myself scarce.* I got up.

'Actually I was just off,' I said. I leaned over and kissed Lucy on the cheek. 'See you soon, Lucy.'

As I walked away I turned back and gave her a look as if to say, 'You're in trouble, girl.' She gave me a half-nod with her chin. She didn't look happy. I carried on my way then turned back after a few moments. It looked like Lucy and Daniel were quarrelling. I felt bad. I didn't want to ruin things for her but it had been dislike on sight with Daniel and witnessing the body language, even from a distance, I could see that Dan the Man was soon going to be history.

Lucy

Lucy's diary

7th September

Full circle. Almost the end of the hols. Can't believe the summer's over. It all goes by too fast. I started off the hols as a singleton and I am a singleton again. So is Izzie. And so is Nesta! TJ's still dating my brother but as Nesta said, just give them time. Cynic. I think they may last quite a lot longer – I've never seen Steve so serious about a girl before.

Nesta got dumped – probably the first time ever. Simon's going to uni soon and he felt that it woudn't be fair to both of them if they were stuck in a long distance relationship. She was pretty cut up about it at first because she knew what he was saying – that he wants to be free to meet other girls. Then Nesta realised that it also meant that she could be free to meet other boys. She's a survivor is Nesta and never stays down for long.

Iz broke up with Ben because she was getting bored of only doing band stuff plus she feels she doesn't want to be tied down just

119

yet. Her and Ben have stayed good mates.

And I dumped Daniel. My first time as a dumper! I felt pretty rotten about it, but that day in Hampstead seeing Dan next to Tony, I just knew that for me there was no comparison. I really didn't like the way he'd been acting over the last week we were together, telling me that I spent too much time with my friends, and he'd get really uptight if I talked on the phone to one of them even for just a minute when he was there – like he wanted my total attention *all* the time. He's been in touch since and even sent flowers and another teddy and I told him to stop. And actually it's been nice to be free to hang out with Izzie, Nesta and TJ again. Tomorrow night we're having a singles only, no boys, survivors' night. Actually one boy is allowed and that's Lal. He confessed to me that he's been in love with Nesta for ages. I really feel for him because I know that Nesta would never fancy him. She likes older boys and Lal just isn't her type. I didn't tell him that, but I did say he could come to the party.

The girls and I all got ready at my house on the night of the party and we had such a laugh when Lal came in dressed in a blond wig, Mum's green silk dressing gown and his face plastered with make-up.

'Hi,' he purred in a girlie voice as he sashayed his way in. 'My name's Lalita. I heard that there was a party going on here.'

'You're right, Lalita,' said Izzie. 'Come right in.'

Lal sat on the bed and crossed his legs gracefully and picked up some nail polish. 'So what do you think? Am I a pink or a mauve kind of girl?'

'I think you're a very *strange* kind of girl,' said Nesta, 'but whatever.'

The party was a total blast. We had invited everyone from our class at school who we knew was single and loads turned up with goodies to eat and CDs to play. We danced around the living room to songs about being single or girl power, sang our lungs out along to 'All By Myself' with Celine Dion – Lal hollering along the loudest. We stuffed our faces with crisps and chocolate then settled down to play party games including Spin the Bottle. There was only one snog forfeit and that was when the bottle pointed to Lal.

'He has to snog Nesta,' I said before anyone else could get in.

She got up and raised an eyebrow at him. 'Think you could take it?' she asked.

His face lit up in anticipation. 'I'll take the chance,' he said.

When they came back from the hall a few minutes later, he had to go and lie down. I swear there were stars and planets circling his head.

At one point, I looked around the room. *This is so easy,* I thought as I watched my mates chat and laugh. *Boys are fun but they can do your head in too.* It had been such a fab evening, all the better for not having to think about what impression I was making on some boy.

'Izzie has written a song,' Nesta announced. 'Come on Iz, sing it for us.'

'Ne-*esta* . . . ' Izzie began to object but everyone started stomping their feet, clapping and calling, 'Izzie, Izzie, *Izzie,*' so she had to get up.

She closed her eyes for a few seconds then began to sing in her lovely, velvety voice.

'I was a broken ship with ragged sails
Now calm waters beckon me
Lying out in warming sun, stretching, feeling free
Waiting for a new wind and a wave upon my bow
Wishing on a rainbow, following my star
Welcoming my new world, I'm going to travel far
Floating in the slip-stream, just going with the flow
Booked a passage on tomorrow with no one else in tow
Floating in the slip stream, just going with the flow.'

I glanced over at Nesta and TJ and they both smiled back at me. Going with the flow. *Yeah, now that sounds good to me.*

Next on the agenda was to watch *Bridget Jones's Diary* so while everyone got settled in on the sofa and cushions on the floor, I got up to clear some dishes away. I was standing at the sink when I thought I saw movement in the garden. It was hard to see because it was dark out there. For a second, I felt a flash of panic and hoped that we weren't going to be bothered by intruders. Sometimes when it got out that someone was having a party, all sorts of nutters turned up. I strained to see and then almost jumped out of my skin when I saw someone's head pop over a bush just beyond the window. It was Tony! He grinned when he saw me, put his index finger up to his mouth as if to say 'Shhh!' and then he beckoned me outside.

I closed the door to the living room then quietly opened the back door, and stepped outside.

'What are you doing here?' I asked.

'Singles' night,' he said. 'I'm single. Why wasn't I invited?'

'No boys.'

'Lal's in there.'

'Yes. He's a token girl for the night.' I glanced back at the house. 'I suppose you could come in, but the girls might kill me for breaking the no-boy rule again after I've already let Lal in.'

'No prob, I only came to see you and . . . ' He put his hand around my waist and pulled me to him. 'Now that we're both single, no ties . . . '

I could feel his warm breath on my face and could smell a slight scent of mint. I couldn't resist and leaned forward at exactly the same time that he did and our lips met, soft then more urgent. It felt wonderful to be kissing Tony again, like I was melting into him and it also felt deliciously wicked to be out kissing a boy on a strictly no-boys evening. We pulled back, looked into each other's eyes and smiled. Out of the corner of my eye, I could see Izzie had come into the kitchen. I pulled Tony away into the shadows. 'You'd better go,' I said.

He nodded then pulled me in for another divine snog.

Izzie opened the back door and called, 'Lucy, where are you? You out there?'

I popped my head out of the shadows. 'Yep, coming. Just putting out some rubbish.'

'Thanks a bunch!' whispered Tony.

I laughed then gave him a push towards the back gate. 'Don't tell Nesta,' I said.

He smiled and gave me a last light kiss on my forehead. 'Our secret,' he said, then disappeared behind the hedge.

Tony

'Are you ill?' asked Nesta when she saw me at my desk in my bedroom. 'You've been in here for hours. It's a gorgeous sunny day outside.'

I indicated all the books. 'I know, but back to school next week and I have a ton of homework I should have done over the hols – and I've got to get good grades.'

'Still want to go to Oxford?'

'Top of my list,' I replied. 'Rob's going for it too.'

'But not for medicine like you are?'

I shook my head. 'He wants to do Classics.'

Nesta laughed. 'Who'd have thought I had a brainbox for a brother?'

'Living proof, my dear sis, that beauty and brains do go together.'

'I'd have thought I was that,' Nesta said and did a twirl.

'Now it's my turn to laugh. Beauty maybe, but brains . . .'

Nesta picked up a pillow from my bed and pounded me

over the head with it. I couldn't let that go so I grabbed one myself and let her have it back. It's Murphy's Law that whenever I rise to the bait of my kid sister, seconds later one of our parents will appear. And this time was no different.

'Tony, leave her alone,' Dad barked as he passed the doorway. 'And Nesta, out and let Tony get on with his studying.'

Nesta got up to leave. 'So what's happening with you and Lucy these days?' she asked.

'I'd have thought that she'd have told you,' I said. 'I thought that you girls talked about everything.'

Nesta shrugged a shoulder. 'Mostly. So are you on or off?'

'What does she say?'

'Nothing. She said something about you being mates. I think that after that creepoid Daniel, she doesn't want a relationship with anyone for a while.'

Cool, I thought, *so she hasn't told about me being in the garden the other night. Excellent. That means she's up for some more secret rendezvous.*

'Ditto,' I said. 'I think we all should have time off for good behaviour. A spell as singletons will do us all good.'

'You *are* ill aren't you?' asked Nesta. 'When have you ever been without a girl or girls in your life?'

I pointed at my books. 'No time for the heart at the mo,' I said. 'Now scoot.'

Nesta left the room and I smiled to myself. Secrets were fun. First Lucy's secret that I was her mystery boy. Then my secret that I knew that I was the boy she fancied – which is still my secret. Maybe one day I'll tell her that I've known all along, but not yet. And now, we have a secret together – that unbeknownst to the others, we will sometimes meet. Nesta was usually the one with the secrets. *So one up on you at last,* I thought as I turned back to my biology book. *And unlike you, sis, I don't blab mine to the world.*

Lucy

Lucy's diary

10th September

Izzie is bonkers at the moment, well more bonkers than usual. First she wanted us all to go and get our belly buttons pierced, which was OK except for the fact that only me and her actually went through with it. I shall innocently flash mine some time when I am over at Nesta's and Tony is there. Nesta went all girlie and pathetic at the tattoo parlour and TJ couldn't risk it seeing as she has Scary Dad as her father.

Izzie's mum went *ballistic* when she found out about the stud. My mum just said that she wants one too. She is as bonkers as Izzie. In fact, sometimes I wonder if Izzie isn't Mum's secret love child.

TJ, Nesta and I are all worried about Iz though. She got off her head the other night at Nesta's. It was quite funny at first when, just for a laugh, we were all sampling the delights of Nesta's parents' cocktail cabinet. I had one called a Screaming Orgasm (just in case I never get to experience the real thing). TJ, Nesta and I had one each, but Izzie kept experimenting and ended up drunk as a sailor behind the sofa, muttering something into the skirting boards about her seeing how mice saw the world.

Tony came back early – I think he knew that we were there and we had a secret snog in the corridor. Feels *très* exciting sneaking out to see him when my mates are in the other room, like we're doing something naughty when actually, we're not really. He was great handling Iz being drunk as a skunk, making her drink loads of water and she might have got away with it if Nesta's parents hadn't arrived home early too, called Izzie's stepfather and then when he arrived, Izzie told him to bog off. Like oops and a half. Nesta got grounded for letting us have alcohol and Izzie's grounded too.

Not sure what's going on with Tony at the mo. I still think about him a lot. He's one of my best friends, who I fancy a bit and snog whenever we're on our own. I wonder if we might ever be proper boyfriend and girlfriend. Izzie has started seeing this boy called Josh who likes to drink and smoke dope. I'm so glad that Tony isn't into all that. We met Josh at one of King Noz's gigs when Izzie was singing and she took a joint and sort of waved it at us, like, 'Look at me the big rebel'. It's like she's pulling away from us and trying to be somebody that she's not. I didn't like Josh very much but it was hard when Izzie asked us all what we thought of him because I remember when I asked my mates what they thought of Daniel. It was hard hearing what they had to say but they were right in the end. And I know we're right about Josh. He isn't good for her. She wrote about him in her diary and her mum read it. We all agreed that was well out of order. Diaries have to be respected no matter how great the temptation to have a nose SO IF ANYONE IS READING THIS, BUTT OUT RIGHT NOW OR THE CURSE OF THE

EGYPTIAN MUMMY WILL EAT YOUR BRAIN OUT WITH A
SPOON ON THE NEXT FULL MOON – AND I MEAN THAT, LAL.

12th September

Izzie has dumped Josh. Huzzah. She also threw up all over him in
the park after she sneaked out late after a gig. Tee hee. He won't
forget her in a hurry! She did see through him though and realised
he was trying to get her sloshed so that he could have his wicked
way with her. What is it with boys and their blooming wandering
hands? Tony has never tried getting me drunk though, but I don't
think he'd ever do anything like that in order to have his wicked way.
Whenever we have talked about going further, he always says he
wants me to feel that the time is right for both of us, which is nice.
Anyway, Josh is history and we're all v. relieved our old Izzie is back.
We had a pizza party to celebrate that and the end of the hols. Year
Ten starts next week. Time seems to be flying by. Eek and er.

Tony

'How long has she been in there?' asked Lucy when I let her in the front door along with TJ and Izzie. They had come straight over after school when I'd called them and were sodden from the rainy skies outside. Lucy looked lovely with her wet hair plastered back from her face. She was definitely getting to me more and more – that or she was getting more attractive.

'Since she got back from the dentist's about an hour ago,' I replied.

'She'll come out when she gets hungry,' said Izzie as she took off her jacket. 'I always do when I've locked myself in my room.'

Lucy and TJ also took off their jackets then the four of us crept down the corridor and positioned ourselves outside Nesta's room. She's a funny girl, my sister. A mass of insecurities that no one knows about. People think that she's mega confident, and some days she is, but other days, she's a lost little girl with no sense of how truly gorgeous she is. Days like today. She came back from the dentist and went to hide in her bedroom, all because she'd had to have a brace put in. I called her mates over to the rescue, plus it was an excuse to see Lucy.

'Come on, let us in,' called Izzie through Nesta's door.

'Yeah, you can't look that bad,' said Lucy.

Nesta wasn't having it so I beckoned them away to rethink the plan. Once in the kitchen, I produced a tin of drinking chocolate, took off the lid then rubbed some on my teeth. They cracked up. It's a trick that Rob showed me. You mush it up, plaster it on your teeth and it makes you look as if you are toothless. We advanced back down the corridor, tin in hand, and at the door, TJ, Izzie and Lucy all applied the drinking chocolate to their teeth. They looked so funny and for a few minutes, none of us could stop laughing. I love making Lucy laugh, she goes all pink and her eyes crinkle up. Nesta unlocked the door. I knew that her curiosity would get the better of her when she heard the commotion. All of us grinned widely at her exposing our darkened teeth.

'All for one and one for all,' said Lucy.

Nesta rolled her eyes, put her hand over her mouth and said, 'Yeah but I've had a brace, it's not that my teeth are rotten!'

'Not yet,' said Izzie, and Nesta had to laugh though she kept her hand up to her mouth. The girls did their best after that to get her to show her brace and eventually after a lot of cajoling, she lowered her hand and let us see.

'*Whoa*,' said Izzie in such a undiplomatic way that I almost burst out laughing, but I held it in because Nesta would have killed me. I glanced at Lucy and mouthed, 'Say something.'

She put her hand on Nesta's arm. 'Did it hurt a lot?'

Nesta nodded and then she was off, happy to be the centre of attention and happy to be with her mates. They are a good bunch and really supportive of each other. I'm still glad that Nesta had got in with them. When TJ, Izzie and Nesta were blabbing, I pulled Lucy away and we went into the kitchen under the pretence of making drinks for everyone. As we always did these days when we were alone, we snuggled together for a sneaky snog. For someone who hadn't kissed a lot of boys, she was very good at it, plus I'd never had as much fun as I was having in my 'non relationship' relationship. After a while, we pulled apart.

'So what are you going to do for your birthday?' asked Lucy.

'Ah. I wanted to talk to you about that,' I said. I was going to be eighteen on September the twenty-second and everyone had been on at me about what I was going to do. 'I asked if I could finally have driving lessons – just about everyone I know has already had them but as soon as I mentioned it, Dad went off on one. No way, he said. I don't understand it.'

'Maybe he'll come around,' said Lucy.

'Doubt it. Mum and Dad gave Nesta and I a talk the other night. Bit broke at the mo – Dad's got a monster tax bill or something – so not only no driving lessons, no big party. Can't say I mind. I'll save the party for when I'm twenty-one. Mum suggested a family dinner, but you know what I'd really like to do?'

Lucy shook her head then laughed. 'No . . . yes, well maybe and I can tell you now that I am *not* going to let you.'

I laughed. 'Not that. No. I told you weeks ago that I would behave and I will. No. I'd like to go for dinner. You and me. Just us. Somewhere romantic.'

'Really?' Lucy blushed and I could see that she was pleased then she made her expression go cool and indifferent. 'I'll see if I can fit you in to my very busy schedule.'

I raised an eyebrow and grinned. 'Yeah right. How about the twenty-third? Day after my birthday?'

Lucy smiled. 'The twenty-third. Hmm. I do believe I might be free. So, OK, yeah. I'll be there.'

Seeing as it was going to be a proper date with Lucy as well as my special occasion, I wanted to get it right so I decided to research a few restaurants to find one with a romantic atmosphere. I reckoned I only needed to have a coffee there to suss it out. First was one at the bottom of Highgate Hill and I went to check it out and asked Nesta to come and give me a second opinion, although I didn't tell her that I was planning to take Lucy there. I arrived late and found Nesta flirting with the waiter, who turned out to be some guy called Luke who she'd met on her acting course. She did her usual showing off and came out with a load of bull about what a great cook she was. I couldn't resist throwing her in it and suggested that seeing as our parents were out the following night, that Nesta cook for him plus Lucy and me. The look on her face was classic. She didn't speak to me all the way home, which for Nesta is really something.

Luke arrived the next night on the dot of seven. I let him in because Nesta was still getting ready in the bathroom. I got him a Coke then the doorbell rang again. I opened the door to find Lucy standing there, a cute grin on her face.

'You look gorgeous,' I said. I took her jacket and leaned in for a quick kiss. 'Smell gorgeous too.'

She blushed a little and looked around. 'Where's Nesta?' she asked.

I jerked my thumb at the bathroom. 'Go on into the living room, Lucy, and meet Luke, he's on his own. I'll be there in a sec.'

I went along the hall and knocked on the bathroom door.

'Do you think that madam might be coming out to greet her guests any time soon?' I asked.

Nesta opened the door and leaned one hand up high on the frame, the other hand on her hip. Very Hollywood.

'One likes to make an entrance,' she said in a movie star voice.

'Sure,' I said, 'just get a move on, your guests are here.'

'And thanks to Mum, I am going to serve a fabbie meal. Luke is going to be so impressed,' she said.

Famous last words, I thought a short time later. Dinner was a total and utter disaster. Hysterical. Mum had helped Nesta earlier in the day and made her famous Jamaican stew. All Nesta had to do was to warm it up, but she even managed to mess that up. She switched the grill on instead of the oven so when it came time to serve up, it was nowhere near hot. We bluffed our way out of it saying that there was a small problem with the electrics, blah de blah de blah. I think Lucy twigged that Nesta had messed up but Luke appeared to fall for it. When he saw that the top of the oven was still working, he came to the rescue and between us we rustled up some pasta.

The evening was back on track. Sort of. Lucy didn't seem very relaxed. Strange because she had been over to our flat a million times for meals and sleepovers – maybe because it was a formal dinner and she wasn't sure how to be with me in public. Like, we were two couples sort of on a date except Lucy wasn't officially my girlfriend.

Things got even more ridiculous when my dingbat of a sister served up creamed cod from the freezer instead of ice cream. Lucy began to relax then and neither of us could stop laughing. The whole evening was fast turning into a farce and I think that Lucy realised that she didn't need to act sophisticated or like a grown up.

Nesta tried her best to ride the storm but later her hair got singed by the candle in the middle of the table. It was one disaster too many, so she ran off to her room to hide. Lucy and I were well tuned in to each other by then and I gave her a quick glance as if to say, 'Go after Nesta,' and she got it immediately and followed her while I did my best to reassure Luke that Nesta wasn't a total nutter, at least not all the time. He didn't seem to mind. He seemed amused by the whole episode.

Lucy got Nesta to come back into the room, and they made some terrible jokes about her being a domestic coddess, and saying, 'Oh my cod!' After that we had a brilliant time with big bowls of real ice cream and all the extras you could pile on: nuts, maple syrup, chocolate sauce. Lucy and I kept catching each other's eye when Luke and Nesta weren't looking. Nice. I felt really close to her and I could see that she felt the same.

When Mum and Dad came home however, things got seriously weird. Dad did a double take when he saw Luke, like he'd seen a ghost. Mum was friendly, chatting away then Dad demanded, 'What's your surname, Luke?'

'De Biasi,' he replied.

Dad's face clouded and he stomped out of the room. I'd never seen him act like that before. Usually he is charming and polite with guests; even Mum looked surprised. I glanced over at Lucy and shrugged. Nesta looked upset. Luke made an excuse and left in a hurry, and Lucy soon followed.

I chased after her and caught up at the gate.

'Thought I'd better make myself scarce,' she said.

'Yeah. I wonder what all that was about. That's not like Dad. Usually he's Mr Charmpants when he meets someone new!'

Lucy looked back inside. 'You'd better make sure Nesta is OK.'

'Will do. Hey, sorry.'

'Not your fault,' she said. 'I had a good time.'

'Me too,' I said and reached out for her hand before turning back to go inside.

Lucy

'But why can't I come over?' asked Izzie. 'I'm so bored. I've done my homework, there's nothing on telly.'

I put on a snuffly voice. 'I've god a reedy bad code, Izzie. You don wadda geddit.'

'You seemed OK at school.'

'I know. Id came on reedy fast. I fee awful.'

'Oh. OK. I'll call Nesta. Hey, get better soon. Inhale some eucalyptus. That will help.'

'Danks Iz.'

I put the phone down and went back to my preparations for my date with Tony. Blue top. Black skirt. Black boots. Pale blue beads. When I was ready, I went downstairs and grabbed my coat before anyone could see that I was dressed up. I'd told Mum that I was going out to watch Nesta and Izzie rehearse a play that they're going to do. Mum came out just as I got my coat on. Phew.

She scrutinised my face. 'You've got a lot of make-up on

for a week night,' she said.

'I'll be mixing with actors, you know what they're like – made-up to the eyeballs. I didn't want to be out of place.'

'Yes but they will be part of the production, won't they? What's the play again?'

'Um . . . *Merchant of Venice.*'

'Oh. One of my favourites. Sure you don't want a lift down there?'

'*No*, Mum. I can get the bus. Bye now,' I blurted and, before she could grill me any more, I opened the door and legged it. *Secret rendezvous aren't much fun when you have the Spanish Inquisition for a mother*, I thought as I made my way to the bus stop. I hadn't liked lying to Izzie either. In my book, mates came first and I had never lied to Izzie, least not about anything major, only wee white lies about how a spot on her chin didn't look too bad when actually it was a monster, stuff like that.

As I sat on the bus, I decided that I didn't want to do the secret rendezvous with Tony any more. I wanted to be able to tell my friends and family what I was doing and what was really going on in my life. The odd secret kiss had been OK, fun in fact, but dating on the sly wasn't my style. I would play along tonight because it was Tony's special birthday dinner, but not again. I felt a twinge of sadness because it might mean that we'd go back to being 'just friends', and I would miss kissing him, but I also knew that if I said that we should come out and be a proper couple, he'd run a mile. With his hang up about commitment, the secret rendezvous thing was a way to be with him which let him feel free plus it avoided any complications arising over the old question of would I or wouldn't I go any further in the bedroom department. But it wasn't working for me any more and if we were ever going to work as a couple, then we both needed to be getting what we wanted. I looked out of the window at the fading sky and thought for the umpteenth time how nice it would have been to talk all this through with Izzie, TJ and Nesta.

Tony

'You do understand why you can't tell anyone about this, don't you?' I asked as we finished our starter. 'It's not just about us meeting in secret, no one must ever know that we came *here* to Biasi's. Dad would go ballistic if he knew that I'd defied him as well as Nesta.'

Lucy nodded. 'I do. Nesta's told me what's been going on.'

'Yeah. It's like a war zone at home with her and Dad arguing. I've never seen Dad being so unreasonable before – but you saw, you were there the first night Dad saw Luke.'

'Will Luke be working here tonight?' asked Lucy.

'No. He does the acting course with Nesta on a Wednesday.'

'She told me that she found out that your dad knew Luke's dad when they were younger.'

'Yeah, they were best of friends apparently, but then Nesta got carried away trying to work out why Dad had fallen out with Mr De Biasi —'

'I know,' Lucy interrupted. 'She told me that she thought

that Luke was your dad's secret love child . . . '

'Yeah and that she'd been snogging her own brother. God, she's priceless. She told me that she decided that Dad had been in love with Mrs De Biasi before he was married and Mr De Biasi stole her from him. None of which was true. But listen, enough about Nesta. I am not going to let her take over my night with you. She gets enough of the limelight as it is.'

I leaned over and took her hand. 'Tonight, my Juicy Lucy, is about us. Let's forget about everything else.' I looked deeply into her eyes and she blushed as the waiter glanced at her and gave her a conspiratorial wink. I love the way she turns pink so easily.

Lucy nodded. 'OK,' she said. 'Let's talk about you. What do you think of me?'

I laughed. 'No, let's not talk about me. Let's talk about you. What do *you* think of *me*?'

Lucy laughed.

It was so easy being with her. We've got each other's sense of humour.

'We'll go out again, won't we?' I asked.

'Um. Yeah.'

'And it's got a nice atmosphere here, hasn't it?'

'Yeah,' said Lucy. 'Is this where you bring all your girlfriends?'

'Only the special ones,' I joked, but this time Lucy didn't laugh. 'You OK?' I asked.

'Yeah. Fine. Um, just thinking about secrets and mates and . . . you know, just thinking.'

Lucy

Lucy's diary

30th September

Too many secrets!

My <u>secret</u> supper with Tony.

<u>Secret</u> snogs with above.

That Tony was my <u>secret</u> mystery contestant. I might tell him one day. Not yet.

A <u>secret</u> part of me wonders if the reason why he wants everything to be <u>secret</u> is because <u>secretly</u> he thinks I am too young for him and fears that *<u>secretly</u>*, so would everyone else.

I'd had enough of all the secrets so told Izzie about my secret meetings with Tony. She laughed her head off. 'I knew, you dingbat,' she said. 'You can't hide anything from me.' Sometimes I think she is a witch. She said that it was her secret that she knew my secret. Hahahahaha – though I didn't tell her about the birthday dinner because I'd promised Tony.

Felt good that Izzie knows. I hated keeping secrets from her more than anyone because we have always shared everything. I asked if she had minded me not telling her and she said that she had in the beginning and would have minded if I had never told her, but now that I had told her, it proved that I trusted her and so everything was cool again. I do love her.

When I told TJ however, she said the opposite of what Izzie had said and that a clandestine affair was the stuff of great romantic novels. Forbidden fruit and all that. She has been reading a book called *Lady Chatterley's Lover* and she said that was all about a secret love affair between a posh lady and her gardener. I hope he was nothing like the man who does our garden. He's ancient with bandy legs.

When I finally told Nesta the truth, she said that she would kill Tony. I had to beg her not to and that if she killed him then she had to kill me too. And then I had to swear them all to secrecy about having told my secret about seeing Tony.

Anyway, I've spent ages trying to decide what to do about Tony. I can't go on as we are because it's doing my head in. Izzie thinks that I should tell him that our relationship should be a 'public' one but I explained to her that no way is he ready for that and he will just freak if I lay my cards on the table. Sometimes I think that I should simply call the whole thing off. At least then I could get on with my life.

Tony

'You serious?' asked Rob as we made our way to the science lab. 'The love meister is actually going to settle down with a girl?'

'He is,' I replied. 'I've been thinking about it for a while now and I reckon the time is right.'

Rob shook his head. 'Never thought I'd see the day.'

'Why not? You and Hannah are going strong, why not me too?' I began to sing. 'Lub is in de air, oobala oobala. Yes. For the first time, I can see the strong points for a steady relationship. Someone to talk stuff over with, do things with and especially at this time with our A-levels – we both have to get our heads down.'

'You sound like an old geezer. What about having a top babe to snog?'

'Yeah, that too. Course. But if I am to get into Oxford, I need top grades. I don't want the distractions of girls who are hyper-emotional, doing my head in with their demands and wanting to talk about their feelings all the time.'

'Sooooo romantic,' said Rob in a tone loaded with sarcasm. 'You like Lucy because she isn't demanding?'

'No, way more than that. I like Lucy because she's cool. She's never done the clingy act. Plus I enjoy her company. She makes me laugh. Anyway, I'm going to tell her next time I see her. We've been sneaking around and nobody really knows that we like each other and are an item. It is time to go public.'

'Poor girl,' said Rob as he opened the lab door as if to let me in, then he tried to trip me up as I walked past him. Luckily I was wise to his pranks and flicked my leg behind his ankle so he almost went over.

Mr Roberts, our science teacher, glanced up and rolled his eyes.

Lucy was waiting for me at the top of the steps outside Highgate tube on Friday after school. She looked pale with the cold, which wasn't surprising because it was freezing, more like February than October, and she only had a jacket on. I took my scarf off when I got to her, wound it around her neck then used both ends to pull her towards me so I could warm her up with a hug. She lurched slightly as if resisting but when I tugged a bit harder, she came forward and let me wrap my arms around her.

After a while I let her go and asked, 'So what's up?'

She grimaced. 'Same ole at school.'

I scrutinised her face. 'That all? You don't look your usual daft self.'

She playfully punched me. 'Let's go and get a drink. I, er . . .

wanted to talk to you about something.'

'Sure,' I said. As we walked over the road to a café, I marvelled at how she was the only girl who ever said something like that and it didn't fill me with dread. Knowing her, she probably did simply want to talk something over. No biggie.

We reached the café and I got us drinks. A cappuccino for me, a blueberry smoothie for Lucy. I took them back to where she was perched on a stool by the window and sat beside her.

'I've got good news,' I said.

'Let's have it,' said Lucy.

'Oxford. Remember I did the entrance exam the other week?'

Lucy nodded.

'I got a place. Well, maybe a place. OK, I have to get five million A stars but that's OK. I'll do it.'

Lucy smiled. 'I'm sure you will. I reckon you could do anything if you put your mind to it.' She looked pleased for me but distracted. Something was going on.

'OK. What is it? Trouble at home?'

Lucy shook her head.

'Mates?'

'Nope. We've all been busy. Nesta's loved up with Luke. TJ's still seeing my brother. All like old married couples. I think Iz would like to meet someone but she's holding out for the right guy. We had a long talk last time we saw each other though about soul mates.'

'What was the verdict?'

'We all thought something different. TJ doesn't believe in them at all. She thinks it's all down to chemistry.'

146

'She would. What about you? What do you believe?'

Lucy shrugged. 'Still thinking about it.'

'Maybe you and me are soul mates? What do you think?' I teased.

Lucy blushed then she looked anxious. 'I . . . thing is . . . um . . . how can I put this?'

Maybe she's sad about the fact that I will be going away to uni in a year, maybe that's it. Yeah, probably is. But a year's a long way off, I thought.

'Are you sad because I will be leaving for uni, is that it?'

She burst out laughing. 'You total bighead.'

'Thank you,' I said and bowed.

'It's not always about you, you know, um . . . though maybe it is sometimes, and . . . it is actually this time.'

'Just spit it out, Lucy,' I said, 'I can tell you're trying to say something and actually I have something I want to say to you too.'

'You go first,' said Lucy.

I shook my head. 'No you. You started it.'

She took a deep breath. 'I . . . I can't go on as we have been. The secrecy and meeting when no one knows. I hate lying to people.'

I smiled, confident in what she was going to say next. That we should be an item. Go public. No wonder she had been nervous. She wasn't to know that I was going to propose the same thing.

'Go on,' I said.

'So . . . I suggest we take a break. As you said, you have your exams to think of and —'

'A break?'

'Yeah. Oh, come on, Tony, don't pretend to be shocked. I know that you don't do commitment and I would never be stupid enough to ask you. You'd run a mile and I don't want to lose you as a friend. So, um, mates. Is that OK?'

'Mates. I . . . '

'What did you want to say?' she blurted.

I had to think fast. 'Exactly the same,' I replied. 'Yes. Exams. Best have no distractions. Yes, I was going to say the same.'

Lucy punched the air. 'I got there first. I win. Yay. Hey, are we a good match or what?'

'The best,' I said. *Drat,* I thought as I sipped my cappuccino. *Guess it's karma. At the beginning of the summer when she came to me thinking it was time to get serious, I blew her off. Now she's doing the same to me. Should I tell her what I really wanted to say?* I watched her drinking her smoothie. *Maybe not. Bad timing. Maybe it wasn't meant to be. Change the subject quick, mate, so she doesn't see that I am lying.*

'So what else is new with Izzie and TJ?' I asked.

Lucy grimaced again. 'Don't know. We've hardly seen each other. TJ's gone down to Devon this weekend. Her sister's getting married so they are talking weddings. She's also been working on the school project about the history of London.'

'Oh yeah, Nesta mentioned it.'

'It's huge, a few schools are joining together for it. TJ's working with Luke, they're doing places of interest. Izzie's doing a bit about the development of religion and I'm doing costume.'

Watching her sip her smoothie and get a milk moustache

made me smile. She was so cute. I didn't want to be just her mate. Maybe I'd risk telling her what I'd meant to after all. 'Actually Luce, I lied.'

She wiped her lip. 'About what? You're not going to Oxford. You're really going to join the foreign legion because I have broken your heart?'

'I will if you won't go out with me. What I was going to say is . . . you, me, let's do it properly. I don't want to take a break. Let's go public. Be a couple.'

She looked shocked. 'As in a *couple* couple? Really?'

'Really.'

'Where's the engagement ring?'

It was my turn to be shocked. Lucy laughed. 'Joking,' she said. 'Got ya.'

I could see that she was chuffed though. Lucy doesn't hide her feelings well. She didn't say anything for a few moments, then she looked me up and down with a disdainful expression. 'Be your girlfriend? Hmm. Let me think about it. Tell you what, I'll get back to you,' she said, then she smiled.

'Thank you, Miss Lovering. I'd appreciate that.'

She slipped off her stool and leaned into kiss me.

Result, I thought.

Lucy

Lucy's diary

5th October

I have a boyfriend. Me. *Moi*. Tony. Me and Tony. Tony and me. I never ever thought I'd write that for certain but he asked. He is. I am. Tadah. I felt like dancing all the way home after he'd asked me, in fact I did when I got to our road. Mrs Cousins over the road saw me and looked at me as if I was a lunatic so I did a quick burst of the Highland Fling for her. It's such a lovely feeling, going to sleep at night and knowing that I will wake up being Tony-the-cutest-boy-in-North-London's girlfriend. Official.

But oh my giddy aunt, other big news. TJ's parents want to move to Devon. We are all well freaked about it, as is TJ. Major trauma, as Nesta said. I would miss her soooooo much. When Candice Carter heard the news, she asked if Steve would be free. I think she was joking. Sure she was joking in fact. Then I said he won't be free because he'll be having a long distance love affair with TJ. Usually TJ would have joined in and seen Candice off, like 'stay away from my man' kind of thing but I noticed that TJ froze. I wonder if her and Steve have had a falling out, but maybe it's because she's so upset about leaving us all. Leaving Steve too. He really likes her. He put himself out to help her on the school project and spent all of the weekend traipsing all over Hampstead to get her shots of the houses where famous people had lived. I've never seen him like this over a girl before. They seem so right together, into the same stuff like books and art. Be fab if they got married and then she'd be my sister as well as my friend. Iz, Nesta and I could be bridesmaids.

School whizzed by after TJ's bombshell, I didn't have time to tell her my news about Tony and I going public. Course I'd told Nesta and Izzie the moment I'd left him at the tube on Friday night. Izzie was well pleased. Nesta was kind of happy for me, but I know she worries about Tony breaking my heart or messing me around. I'm the same about Steve and TJ so I can't object.

In the meantime, Tony and Lucy. Lucy and Tony. It's true. It's official. Yahey.

Tony

'So how's it going with Lucy?' Rob asked a couple of weeks later when he was round at my place having an after-school milkshake.

'Good. Better than good,' I said as I chopped bananas into the mix. We were a proper couple, seen out in public, acknowledged as Tony and Lucy. Lucy and Tony. It felt good – like getting a present you've wanted for ages and then it's finally yours.

'First base? Second base? Or have you got a home run and done the deed?'

I tapped my nose. 'A gentleman doesn't kiss and tell.'

Rob laughed. 'So you have done it. You ole dog. *AWOOOO.*'

I didn't say anything. I hadn't even got past first base with Lucy and I didn't want to push her. I wanted it to be right. I wasn't going to tell Rob that though. No point in ruining the legend that is my love life.

Lucy

I peeked out of the window. It was cold and bleak out there, the trees bare against a December sky. I got dressed and went down for breakfast.

Steve was already down. He looked his usual miserable self.

'Uh,' I said to him. I knew how to speak his language.

'Uh,' he replied without looking up.

I poured some muesli into a bowl and sat at the table. Moments later, Lal burst in. 'Is that for real?' he asked.

'What for real?' I asked.

'That email from TJ?'

'To who? To me?' I asked. 'Have you been looking at my mail?'

'Not yours, dingbat,' said Lal. 'On ours.' (Steve and Lal share a PC upstairs.)

Steve flushed slightly. 'Have you been looking at my private email?'

'I have. I wasn't snooping. I —'

'Yeah right,' Steve interjected, then he turned to me. 'You might as well know, Lucy. TJ dumped me. I got an email from her.'

'Dump you by email? She wouldn't.'

'Well she did.'

'Can I go and see?'

Steve shrugged. I got up and ran up the stairs to the boys' room and looked on the computer. And there it was.

From: babewithbrains@psnet.co.uk
To: jamesblonde@psnet
Date: 12th December
Subject: Us

Dear Steve

I am writing to tell you that I can't go out with you any more. I'm really sorry and I hope that you won't be too upset. It's not you. I think you're fantastic. It's me. But I'm not going to insult you by explaining or trying to make excuses. It's never easy ending something and I'm keeping this short as it's about the hundredth version I've written and I couldn't find the right words in any of them.

I hope that you will always be my friend as you genuinely do mean a lot to me and I really enjoyed going out with you and I am sorry to do this by email, but will explain why I had to do this later.

Your friend
TJ

His friend? I thought. *She was supposed to be my friend too. One of my best friends. What the heckity thump is she up to?* I raced downstairs.

'I am so sorry, Steve, I knew nothing about this,' I said.

'It's not on, dumping someone by email,' said Lal through a mouth of toast. 'Totally out of order.'

'Yeah? Since when have you been Mr Sensitivity? You OK, Steve?' I asked.

Steve shrugged again. 'Uh,' he replied. I didn't press him any more because Mum came in and if she got wind of what had happened, she'd make a big fuss and try to get him to talk about it and I wasn't about to do that to Steve. I no longer felt like breakfast. I needed to get to school and find out why TJ had done this. *She'd better have a good explanation,* I thought as I put my jacket on. Although Steve and I didn't talk much, he was my brother and I hated to see him hurt.

Tony

School has been full on this term and I put my key in the door to our flat with relief. The weekend was here and I was going to relish every moment, starting this evening with a date with Lucy. I was even thinking of testing the water to see how she felt about taking our relationship to the next level.

I threw my coat over to the rack in the hall. *Drat.* It missed. *Must be losing the old touch,* I thought as I picked it up from the floor and hooked it up properly. I went through to the kitchen to make a tuna melt sarnie and there were Nesta and Lucy sitting at the breakfast bar.

I went over and gave Lucy a hug then tried to wrestle her off her stool. She shoved me away. 'Get off, Tony.'

'You know you want me,' I said, then I let her go and turned to Nesta. 'Mum or Dad home?'

She shook her head. 'Mum left money for a take away if you fancy.'

'Cool. Later? What do you fancy?' I said as I went to the fridge.

'Nothing,' said Nesta. 'I am never going to eat again.'

I stopped for a moment and looked at the pair of them. Lucy pulled a glum face. *Trouble,* I thought.

'I see. So spill, what's happened?'

Nesta sighed and stared at the floor. 'Only the worst day of my whole life,' she said in a wobbly voice.

I glanced over at Lucy.

'Want me to tell him?' she asked Nesta.

Nesta nodded and sighed again. She can really ham it up on the drama queen front when she wants. 'May as well,' she said. 'The whole world will know soon.'

'TJ has been two-timing —' Lucy started.

'With Luke,' Nesta interrupted.

'TJ? Luke? *Your* Luke?' I asked. 'Luke De Biasi. No way.'

Nesta nodded. 'My friend. One of my best friends. Can you believe it? With *my* boyfriend! She even had snog rash this morning from snogging him.' She sighed again and took a big gulp of air.

'*And* she dumped Steve,' I added. 'By email.'

I sat on a stool. 'Whoa. Pretty major, huh?'

Lucy nodded. 'You can say that again. We can't believe it. Plus that's not all. She'd told Izzie but she hadn't told us. Us. Her best mates. We tell each other everything. That's one of our rules.'

I nodded. 'Not good. Not good. You OK, Nesta?'

'Do I *look* as if I am OK?' she blurted. 'No. I am not. I have been cheated on by a mate. I really liked Luke too.' Another

157

gulp of air and she put the back of her hand up to her forehead to complete the tragic look. 'I don't know who I can trust any more.'

Normally I would have tried to tease her when she does her drama queen routine but I could feel anger rising from the pit of my stomach. No one did this to my sister. I wanted to find Luke De Biasi and punch his lights out.

'Where is he?' I asked.

'Luke?' asked Nesta. 'Don't know. With TJ? Snogging TJ?'

'No. He's probably working at his dad's restaurant,' said Lucy. 'Why?'

I got up. 'I have something to say to Luke De Biasi,' I said and I punched my fist into the palm of my other hand.

Nesta and Lucy exchanged worried looks.

'No. *No*, Tony, you mustn't,' said Lucy.

'She's right,' said Nesta. 'We don't want you hurt too.'

'You saying I couldn't take him on?

'*No,*' said Nesta. 'No, course not. Just we've got enough to think about as it is without worrying about stupid boys punching each other too – so just leave it, will you? In fact, I don't want to think about it any more at all. It's giving me a headache.'

I glanced at Lucy. She nodded. 'I think I need to stay with Nesta tonight, don't you?'

Nesta slumped forward. *Bummer,* I thought. *That's my night ruined.* It was definitely not the night to be encouraging Lucy to go to second, third or any base. I could punch Luke for that alone, never mind for cheating on my sister. I knew there was no point in trying to persuade Lucy because I knew how intense these girls were about their friendships and being there for each other when in need, and for that reason, I also knew that Nesta would be cut up about TJ as much as Luke. What a creep.

I guess people can say the same about me, probably have done in fact. I'd two-timed many a girl in the past – a trail of broken hearts behind me, that's part of my legend. No way was I a creep though – my attitude had been that all was fair in love and war. But Nesta looked well cut up. I didn't like to think I'd done that to anyone. I felt confused. Part of me wanted to let Luke have it. Another part of me understood his behaviour completely.

Lucy

Lucy's diary

18th December

Holy moley, lemon joley. Phew, what a mad time these last few weeks have been. The maddest ever – and seeing as it's coming up to Christmas, it ought to have been our best time instead of weeks of misery. Nesta and I had a big falling out with TJ and Izzie after we found out that TJ was a two-timing love rat. Even though it wasn't Iz who was the two-timer, I had believed that she told me everything. I am her oldest mate after all. It was awful seeing them at school and it being so weird with them. I missed them so much even though I hated them. Then Izzie emailed me to say that TJ backed out of the project because she didn't want to see Luke any more.

And then at the beginning of this week, TJ comes into school and confronts all of us. Said she never meant to hurt Nesta and that Luke had been lying to everyone behind their backs telling Nesta one thing and her another, and that Nesta had to know the truth about him. She also said that she wanted to be mates with us more than be with someone like Luke. She practically got down on her knees and begged. I could see that she was really upset and even though I was mad with her for hurting Steve, I felt for her too. I decided to be friends again and I believed what she said about Luke stringing her along. Nesta took a while longer, but she came around too and already she has seen someone new that she likes. It was hysterical. It was at the final day of the project and we were all at the display and this gorgie guy came in and we all clocked him and had such a laugh, he clocked Nesta though, which none of us minded because she needed a boost to her confidence. Luke was there too. He looked terrified when he saw us all together, mates for ever, united – and thank goodly goodness, we really are friends again. I know some girls put boys first and drop their friends but Nesta, Izzie, TJ and I know that boys come and go, but friends are for ever.

Tony and I are great. Still a regular couple with regular dates, regular phone calls – he calls most evenings after school just to catch up and most weekends we do a movie or get a DVD and a pizza round at his place. Kind of weird being a proper couple, nice though, except for going shopping with him. That's a big no no. We tried one afternoon and did my favourite shops in Hampstead. I soon realised that mooching around clothes shops and trying stuff on is much more fun with my girlfriends. Tony couldn't fake it – despite trying to be enthusiastic, I could see that he was bored out of his mind. Top points for effort though.

I made him a calendar for Christmas. I collected all the photos we have had taken of us since I have known him, like the one the waiter took of us at Biasi's just after his birthday, that will be the picture for September. Steve helped me put them against a background right for that month, like against a snowy scene for

December and against a sizzling hot beach for July. Hope he likes it. The girls all think it's fab and Izzie wants to do one of us mates too. Steve said he'd do one of us for my birthday in May. He's been really quiet these past weeks. I think he took being dumped hard. His pride was hurt and he retreated into himself. He's better recently and is being pursued by a girl called Gina. It's perked him up no end.

Tony keeps teasing that what he wants for Christmas is to take things a stage further in the oo la la department. Not sure what to do. Oo la la and oo er.

Tony

I threw my book to the bottom of the bed. 'Work, work, work. That's all I ever do.'

Lucy picked the book up and glanced at it for a moment. 'Bo-oring,' she said and tossed it aside too. We were top to tail. Her propped up at the end of the bed reading one of her glossy mags and me at the top, supposedly studying. I had been going at it for weeks, even over Christmas *and* New Year, although we did manage to get in a few parties, but most of January had been nothing but studying. I was determined to get A stars all the way and that meant maximum effort for all of my last year.

Lucy got up and went to the calendar that she had given me for Christmas. It had pride of place over my desk area and had pics of Lucy and I in various scenarios for every month. My fave was the May one when we were two faces amongst a hundred sheep in a *Where's Wally?* type of pic.

'So when is your first exam?' asked Lucy as I got up and

walked to the window. Outside it was dark and dreary. Typical February weather.

'Too blooming soon,' I replied. 'Biology is first. Oh God, I wish I was going on holiday somewhere.'

'Me too. Our school is doing a school trip to Florence at half term. I so wish that I could go.'

'Oh yeah, Nesta mentioned it. I think Mum said she could go.'

Lucy sighed. 'Izzie and TJ too. I'll be the only one left behind. I've asked but Mum and Dad just can't afford it.'

'That sucks,' I said, then I went back to the bed and slid behind Lucy so that she was between my knees. I nuzzled her neck. 'So we will just have to think of things to do to make up for being left behind, hey?' I was about to try my luck and see if I could get past first base. I had to play it really carefully because sometimes she slapped me right away, other times she seemed to be more into it. She'd been slightly less resistant lately. Just as she turned and we were mid-snog, Mum burst in.

'Whoa, oops, sorry to disturb, Tony. Hi Lucy. Didn't realise you were still here. Um. Right,' she blustered. She looked embarrassed at first then concerned. *Oh no,* I thought, *I hope she's not going to get Dad to give me another sex talk later.* Whenever I have a girl in my room, they feel the need to give me a caution. Last time was hysterical. Dad said we needed to have a talk about sex. I replied, 'OK Dad, any time, just let me know what you need to know.' Nesta had cracked up.

'Right Lucy,' continued Mum. 'Isn't it time you were getting off home?'

Lucy had gone bright red. She sprang off the bed. 'Yes. Of

course. Right. See ya, Tony.'

I pulled her hand and made her sit down. 'We weren't doing anything, Mum, if that's what you think. Lucy's going to be a nun, aren't you Luce? She's promised to God.'

Lucy went even redder.

'Just be careful, that's all,' said Mum and she backed out of the room.

Lucy and I looked at each other then burst out laughing.

Lucy

'It's your decision, Lucy,' said Steve.

It was one of the rare occasions when my brother had decided to communicate. We were at home alone one night after school and had bonded over a tub of Ben and Jerry's Chunky Monkey ice cream. Having a proper conversation happened with Steve about once a year. Lal and I had a joke that he was like a exotic flower that bloomed occasionally and you had to make the most of it when he opened up. We'd been talking about Lal, who had got a mysterious letter to go and see a solicitor – something to do with our neighbour Mrs Finkelstein. She was a weird old stick, angry with everyone and we were worried that Lal had done something stupid to annoy her and had got into trouble. Somehow we'd moved on to talking about relationships and doing 'the deed'.

'Have you done it?' I asked.

Steve tapped his nose. 'None of your business,' he said.

Open, but not that much, I thought, then decided that

actually I didn't want to know. The thought of either of my brothers having sex made me feel weird although I knew that Lal was still a virgin simply because even if he snogs a girl, he has to announce it to the world.

'I know it's my decision,' I said. 'I have been thinking about it.'

Steve looked at me with a concerned expression. 'You do know that you're underage, don't you?'

I shrugged. 'So are loads of people in our school that have done it. So?'

'It's against the law. We had some guy come into our school and give us the lecture about the legal age, which is *sixteen*, in case you didn't know. That and the condom talk.'

'Yuk.'

'Hmm, well, they say if you're not ready to talk about it, you're not really ready to do it. Anyway, lots of people lie about what they say they've done.'

'Yeah, yeah. Besides, I'll be fifteen in May, that's almost sixteen.'

Steve raised an eyebrow.

'But what do you think?' I asked. 'Should I do it?'

'Jeez. *I* don't know Lucy. I'm your big brother! I don't really want to think about it. Talk to Tony.'

I rolled my eyes. *No point in that,* I thought, *I know what he'd say. Wahey and get your kit off.* I had pretty well decided that I was going to go further. I liked, no, *loved* Tony and I think he felt the same although he had never actually said the l-word. I hadn't said it to him either. I didn't want to scare him off. We had been going steady and that was really something for him.

He would be responsible if I agreed to do it, I'm sure he would. I had talked it over with the girls and they were surprised. None of us had done it yet and, not that it's a competition, I don't think anyone thought it would be me who was first. What's worrying me is that a girl in our year at school got pregnant. I saw her crying in the cloakroom and saw how freaked out she was. 'Candice Carter is pregnant,' I blurted out to Steve.

'That redhead in your class? She was here for your singles only party last summer, wasn't she?'

I nodded. 'Yeah. She's a laugh normally, but I've never seen her so upset, like all her plans for the future have disappeared, and it made me think.'

'Yeah, but not every girl who has sex gets pregnant, Luce. Especially if you take precautions.'

'I know but some do and no contraceptive is a hundred per cent guaranteed.'

Dad arrived back moments later so that put the kibosh on our conversation. Having the sex conversation is not one I wanted to have with him again. Once was enough. He'd sat me, Steve and Lal down and gave us a lecture like we knew nothing and as if we don't go over it all at school. We had all dutifully sniggered like five-year-olds. Still, Candice's situation had made me question my decision to go ahead with Tony. Having sex, even with precautions, was, as my brother had kindly pointed out, illegal, as well as being a risk. Was it one that I was seriously ready to take?

Tony

Nesta knocked on the door. 'You OK in there?'

'Fine, yes, thanks.'

'Lucy in there with you?'

I opened the door and Nesta looked past me and tried and get into the room. 'Where is she?'

'Gone,' I said and gently shoved her out then shut the door.

'OK, be like that, rude person,' Nesta called back through the door.

I wasn't in the mood for Nesta. If she got the slightest inkling of what had just happened, she'd want every detail and then no doubt she'd blame me. It was Saturday night. Mum, Dad and Nesta had been out all evening and Lucy had been over. I thought it was to be *the* night. She'd been dropping hints and when she arrived, she was giving me all the signals. It was going great at first and it looked like we were even going to get past second base and maybe on to third then she suddenly pulled back and told me about some girl in her class that had got pregnant. I did my best to reassure her that it wasn't going to happen to us and I backed off a bit. When we started kissing again the moment had gone. She tried to get into it, but I could see that she had panicked and was anxious, maybe not doing it for the right reason. I got the feeling that she was trying to do it because she felt that she ought to rather than wanted to – and I didn't want that. In the end, she admitted she wasn't ready and before I could stop myself, it was out of my mouth that maybe we should take a break. I mean, although she's almost fifteen, I'm eighteen. I have had more experience than her and if I was honest with myself, holding back from going further with Lucy was doing my head in. No way did I want to rush her though. I wanted her to want it too, as much as I did, but tonight, I realised that we were poles apart and I began to think that maybe the age difference was the problem. So we agreed to finish. It was awful, she looked so hurt.

After she'd gone, I picked up the phone a few times to say, no, let's carry on as we were but I put the receiver back down. I knew it was for the best – but that didn't stop me feeling totally crapola about it.

Lucy

Mum and Lal looked decidedly suspicious when I got home from school. It had been a rubbish day. I'd been worried about Lal because I knew he had his appointment with the solicitor, plus I felt crap and a half about breaking up with Tony. I was going to miss him so much. I had loved being his girlfriend and I liked the way he called me every night. It already felt like there was a big empty space in my life. The girls had been supportive as ever, Nesta wanting to go and kill Tony of course (again) so I had to talk her out of it (again) but we did have a laugh about ways to get revenge – Izzie took the prize with her idea to sneak into Tony's bedroom and sew prawns into his bedding. Snicker snicker. But I didn't really feel like laughing. I didn't really want to take revenge. It wasn't like that with us. I still cared about him a *lot*, I couldn't deny it, and the fact that Izzie, Lucy and TJ were soon about to take off for Florence wasn't helping either.

'What's going on?' I asked as soon as I saw that Mum and Lal were home.

Mum told me to call everyone together in the kitchen and I felt a rush of panic as I went upstairs to call Steve and Dad down. We only had family talks like she was proposing when something serious was going on.

'Right,' said Mum when we had all gathered. 'Everyone's here. Anyone want a cup of tea?'

'*Mum,*' I groaned. 'If you wait another second, I swear I am going to explode.'

'OK. What do you want first?' Mum asked. 'The good or the bad news?'

'Bad news,' said Dad. 'Let's get that over with.'

'OK,' said Mum. 'The bad news is that Mrs Finkelstein died just after Christmas.'

Lal couldn't contain himself any longer. 'And the good news is that she left *me* some money.'

As soon as he'd told us how much, what he intended to do with it and we'd picked ourselves up off the floor, I raced to the phone and had to wrestle Steve for it. I won!

I called Nesta first. 'Oh my gorgonzola. I am coming to Florence!' I blurted. 'Some old dear left Lal some dosh for being kind to her cat and he's going to give each of us two grand. Two grand! Yabadabadoodah. Mum and Dad said I can come to Florence with you guys. Oo, what to wear? OK, got to go, got to tell the others immedi-issimo.'

Blissimo, I thought as I hung up and dialled Izzie's number. *Just goes to show in life that you never know what's around the next corner. Life can be rubbish one minute then something amazing happens.*

Tony

It was half term and I was working on the computer when the photographs from Nesta in Italy came through. The girls had been gone just for a few days and apart from one call from Nesta to say that she'd arrived safely, we had heard nothing. Not that Mum and Dad were worried. They knew that there were teachers on the trip too. I had hoped that Lucy might have got in touch. I had been missing her and had begun to regret the night when we broke up. I was beginning to think that I'd rather be with her with no 'extra-curricular activity' than without her. I kept remembering how upset she'd looked the night we'd finished and I hoped that it hadn't overshadowed her Italian trip, although I had a feeling that it might have done. She was clearly well cut up.

I pressed the button to open the pictures and, as they began to download on to my computer, my phone bleeped that I had a text. I glanced at it to see who it was from. Andrea Morton, again. Pretty, slim, long blond hair, great body, seventeen and a laugh. Old mate of Hannah's. We almost got it together last summer at a barbecue. I'd meant to get in touch, but never got round to it because she lives in Brighton now so she wasn't exactly on my radar, and then Lucy happened.

Andrea's text was an invite to go to a rock weekend down near her. I was tempted. Apparently her parents were away. Rob and Hannah had already gone, but I'd stayed behind to get ahead with work. However, I'd been studying for days and was beginning to get brain overload – like I was reading the pages, but it wasn't going in.

I was about to text back *Maybe next time* (no harm in keeping the door open) when I glanced at the photos on my screen. I smiled when I saw pics of Izzie larking about doing a Buddha pose on a bed. *Looks very posh for a school trip dorm,* I thought as I looked at the plush room she was in – like some really posh hotel. Next was a pic of Nesta in her dark glasses sprawled across the bed with a cocktail glass in her hand. *Typical Nesta,* I thought. *Probably got in with some rich tourists and blagged her way into their rooms.* And then there she was. Lucy, pictured peeking out from behind a curtain, and then . . . I froze. *What? Who?* Photos of Lucy appeared with some tall blond guy. He was clearly well into her because he was kneeling at her feet with a stupid rose in his mouth, looking up at her adoringly and she was grinning like an idiot, clearly not missing me one bit. A couple more pics came through. None of Izzie or TJ or Nesta, just Lucy and the boy. I felt gutted and wasn't sure if I was mad jealous or just mad mad that I'd been sitting here moping when the rest of the world was out having a life. I wondered if Nesta had sent the photographs on purpose – as if to say, 'Lucy's moved on, so should you.'

Message received and understood, I thought as I picked up my phone to send Andrea a reply to her invite. *I've been an idiot sitting here thinking that Lucy has been out there pining over me when actually it was me pining over her. Well, not for much longer. I'm nobody's sucker. Brighton and Andrea, here I come.*

Lucy

Lucy's diary
25th February

I am writing this on the plane coming home from Florence, Italy, Earth, the universe, etc, etc. I have had an unforgettable week. Italy is gorgissimo. We did all the sites, the Duomo (puff puff, about a million steps to get to the top), the Uffizi (loads of art, loads of tourists trying to see the art and me being short had to peer through people's armpits in order to see anything), the Ponte Vecchio (loads of shops, need loads of money), Palazzo Vecchio (loads of painted walls). So – lots of art, lots of great ice cream, lots of marble statues with bare bottoms – and their willies showing too. Oo er. The most famous is David by Michelangelo, he is fit and a half. Great bum. All very stunning, but as Izzie said by the end of it, we were totally frescoed out – we've decided to say that in future instead of freaked out – like, I'm so frescoed out about . . .

Best of all though, I had a holiday romance with an American boy called Teddy who is a bit of a Michelangelo masterpiece himself

– but a clothed one. We had our first kiss in Fiesole, a village up on the hill overlooking Florence. It was soooo romantic and I shall remember it and him for ever. I hope he writes and stays in touch. I think he will. One of the reasons that it was so great to hang out with him was because he took my mind off Tony and showed me that there are other boys that I fancy and there will be other boys that I have strong feelings for and boys who can show me different aspects of life. I guess like Nesta has always said, there are lots of different types of fruit in the basket and no one can say that one is better than the other, they're just different. It's like that with boys – pears, oranges, melons, mangoes and some that are plain bananas! All different. Back in the UK, I was beginning to think that Tony was the only one I would ever feel anything for. But now I feel renewed and refreshed and ready to start again. A life without Tony. Tadah.

Izzie had a holiday romance too, with a gorgeous Indian boy called Jay. I think they will be an item when they get to the UK. Nesta got off with an Italian boy called Marco on the last night, it wasn't exactly a holiday romance but a bit of fun. TJ was the only one of us who didn't get off with anyone. She met a guy called Liam who was into her, but she didn't fancy him. I think she still has feelings for Luke although she doesn't say much and —

'WARGH!' I cried as the plane took a sudden dip. Seconds after came an announcement that we had hit some turbulence and should fasten our seat belts. That put a stop to my writing. The plane lurched again and someone screamed at the back of the cabin as the plane shuddered. The next twenty minutes were pure hell. Everyone looked well frescoed out as the plane bounced around in the air, even the air hostesses looked worried – one sat in a seat behind us and we could hear her swearing under her breath.

Izzie leaned forward from the seat behind. 'Hold hands,' she insisted. Izzie, Nesta, TJ and I grabbed hands and encouraged each other to stay calm. Izzie suggested begging or praying. TJ suggested song lyrics for plane crashes, like *Ah, ah, ah, staying alive.* All I could think was *Please God, let us land safely, and please let me see my mum and dad, brothers and Tony. Please, please let me see Tony again.*

Tony

The sun was shining, cold and bright and Andrea was waiting for me at the train station with Rob and Hannah by the ticket desk as we'd arranged. *Just what the doctor ordered,* I thought as she linked her arm through mine. She looked good in a three-quarter-length velvet coat, skinny jeans and long blond hair flowing loose past her shoulders. I noticed a couple of guys checking her out, but she only had eyes for me. We caught a bus to her house so that I could dump my stuff and, once there, I saw that it was understood that I'd be sharing with her because Rob was in with Hannah in the spare room. *Can do,* I thought as I left my stuff on Andrea's bedroom floor next to the sleeping bag that had been laid out for me, not that I thought I'd be actually sleeping in it, judging by the flirty glances that Andrea had been giving me. The house wasn't far out of town, a big place, detached in acres of garden, and the venue where the music was happening was a stone's throw away. All very comfy cosy.

The gig was rocking when we got there, three floors with a few different bands in what used to be a textile warehouse but was now empty apart from events like this. The rest of the day passed in a pleasant haze of music. We drifted around like everyone else, going from room to room listening to who was on, eating whatever took our fancy from the stalls located in various corridors which sold all sorts – from berry smoothies and alfalfa sprout salads to greasy burgers and chips. It felt great to be away from my books, chilling with a top-looking girl on my arm. Some of the bands in the smaller rooms were dire, but the act on the main stage on the ground floor was the business. Circle of Five topped the bill and the lead singer was a brilliant performer, dancing between three mikes and giving it his all vocally. After they'd finished, we had a few drinks at the bar then made our way back to Andrea's place.

'Um. I'm going to keep some clothes on,' I said as I snuggled down into the sleeping bag. It was a chilly night and the house was cold after the heating had gone off. It wasn't long before Andrea had snuggled in besides me. I knew she would – either that or she'd invite me into her bed, but the floor was fine by me. I obliged by cuddling her back. After having held myself back with Lucy, I was well ready for a girl who wasn't going to change her mind at the last minute, and, from the signals Andrea had been giving me all day, it was party time. We kissed and fooled around for a while and she began to nuzzle into my neck and . . . I just couldn't get into it. I tried again. It felt flat. She felt wrong. She smelled wrong and although there was nothing actually wrong with her and her perfume was OK, it was just . . . *How does that song go?* I asked myself. *Dad's always playing it . . . by some old geezer?* *'Though your lips are lovely, they're the wrong lips.'* I wanted Lucy. Lucy's lips. She'd got me. Even at thousands of miles away, I could feel her pulling me. What I had with her was for real.

'What's the matter?' asked Andrea.

I gently pushed her away.

'It's not you, it's me,' I said.

She sighed. 'That old line.'

'I know. I'm sorry. Just . . . I've been involved with someone lately and . . . this just doesn't seem right.'

'Am I hearing right? The love meister's in love?' she asked, then laughed. 'Don't think I don't know your reputation. You never stay with one girl for long.'

'So many girls, so little time,' I quoted one of my favourite lines.

'So why not you and me?'

'It wouldn't be fair on you, Andrea. And I do like you, I really do . . . '

'Just you like this other girl more,' she finished for me.

I paused a minute. I hadn't even realised myself. 'I guess I do,' I said.

Andrea snuggled in again and gave me a hug. 'She's a lucky girl then whoever she is,' she said, then she crawled out of the bag and into her own bed. 'Night, Costello.'

'Night, Morton,' I replied. 'Bad timing, hey?'

'Sure,' she said.

She was cool. Shame. So many girls, only one for me. As I fell asleep, I decided that it wasn't over with Lucy and I. Not by a long shot. I wasn't going to admit defeat just because of a photo of some bloke she had only just met over in Italy.

A few days later, I arrived at the airport half an hour before Lucy's plane came in to land. I browsed the shops looking for the best flowers then finally settled for two dozen white roses. I had a cup of coffee then, flowers in hand, I went to stand near the arrival doors. As I was making my way there, two blonde girls spotted me.

'And what have you done, you naughty boy?' asked one with a cheeky grin.

The other linked her arm through mine. 'Never mind her. Are those for me?'

I grinned at both of them. 'I haven't done anything, I've been a good boy —'

'Yeah right,' said the taller of the two.

I smiled again. 'Honest.'

The arrival board said that the flight from Florence had landed so I positioned myself near the doors where she would be able to see me when she came through. As I waited, I felt a sudden flood of doubts. *You idiot,* said a voice in my head. *She may have another boyfriend by now – the one in the photo. What if he's with her? What if he was on the same flight? How's it going to look? Me standing here like a dodo with a bunch of flowers. She might think I am a total loser. Maybe I should go now before I make a fool of myself.*

The doors opened and people began to come through: an old man, a young couple, a girl in black – very Italian sophisticated – then I spotted someone from Lucy's school, then a bunch of them, then there she was – Lucy. She was pushing a trolley and talking to Izzie, Nesta and TJ were behind. *Phew, no sign of the blond boy,* I thought. I felt myself beginning to grin from ear to ear when the girls looked over. I put the flowers up so they couldn't see my face then peeked through. They were all staring and then Lucy realised that it was me. I needn't have worried about her reaction. She abandoned the trolley, ran over and literally leaped at me. She hugged me with tears in her eyes.

'Wow, so you missed me, huh?' I asked.

'No. Crap flight,' she said. '*Really* crap flight. God, it's *so* good to see you. It's so good to be on the ground. I thought I might never see you again.'

I laughed. She missed me all right.

Seconds later, Nesta came and flung herself at me too. 'Ohmigod, Tony. We almost *di-ed.* It was the *worst* moment of our whole lives.'

By this time, TJ and Izzie had caught up and joined in the group hug too. 'We're so glad to be on the land,' said TJ. 'I swear, everyone got off that flight with their hair standing on end like Marge Simpson, it was so freaky out there.'

Izzie giggled. 'We were *so* frescoed out.'

And then they all started giggling, then hugged me again.

At that moment, the two blonde girls who had commented earlier on the flowers walked past.

'Hey, naughty boy,' the tall one called. 'You're popular. What is it? Your aftershave?'

I grinned over at them. 'Just natural charisma, darling, some of us got it, some of us ain't.'

Lucy

The group hug at the airport with Tony didn't last long because Mrs Elwes, our art teacher, came through the arrival doors soon after and ushered us girls on to the coach. We all pleaded for Tony to be able to come too and when she realised that he was Nesta's brother, she relented. It was hysterical. He was totally in his element to be surrounded by so many girls and of course, they were all checking him out and looking well impressed. I felt so chuffed that he was so clearly with me because as soon as we were all on the coach, he beckoned me to go and sit with him at the back.

'Missed you, Lovering,' he said as he put his arm around me and gave me the lightest of kisses on my lips.

'Me too,' I said, though it was a lie. I hadn't exactly missed him until I thought that the plane was going down because there was so much happening and of course Teddy had been a major distraction. 'How was the weekend in Brighton?'

'How did you know about that?'

'Nesta. Think your mum told her where you were when she called home one night.'

He took my hands and we linked fingers. 'Brighton? Hmm. Interesting,' he said and gave me an enigmatic smile. I wasn't going to ask. I knew he had been with a girl. 'And how was Florence?'

'Hmm. Also interesting,' I replied and gave him what I hoped was an enigmatic smile back. *Two can play at that game,* I thought. He grinned back at me because he knew I'd got him. We didn't get much chance to talk after that because Mrs Elwes had clocked that we were at the back on our own, so she called Nesta to go and sit with us. She came to join us, along with Izzie and TJ, and we spent the rest of the coach ride filling him in on the sights we'd been to see. He held my hand all the time though.

Mum was waiting to collect Izzie and I once we'd got back to the school, and Nesta's dad was waiting for her. He seemed surprised to see Tony there with us. We unloaded our cases and bags and as everyone dispersed, Tony pulled me aside.

'Catch you later?' he asked. 'Call me when you've settled in.'

I nodded.

'Wow, what's come over him?' asked Izzie. 'He's come over all Mr Keen.'

And Mr Keen he was. He turned up just after supper. I hadn't called him because I was feeling queasy and had gone up to bed early. It might have been due to the landing, but it might also have been due to a bout of food poisoning that I'd had in Florence.

Tony sat on the end of my bed.

'It's not catching,' I said. 'I think it was a dodgy prawn I had in Italy.'

Tony nodded. 'Ah yes, for we are all prawns in the chess game of life, are we not?'

'Very funny,' I said. 'Prawns in the cocktail of life.'

We sat in an amiable silence for a while then Tony got up and began to pace the room. 'So, Lovering. What next?' He pointed at himself then at me.

'I thought we'd agreed: friends,' I said.

Tony grimaced. 'What if I wanted more?' he began.

I pulled the duvet up to my neck and put on a prissy girlie voice. 'But that's aways the probwem, you are a naughty naughty boy and I am a chaste ickle girl.'

Tony smiled and came and lay next to me. I shoved him off and he landed on the floor with a thump.

'Some girls would love to have me on their bed,' he said.

'And in it,' I replied and then I realised that he had been serious. He was saying that he wanted us to get back together. I wasn't ready. I still wasn't ready. Not to go further in the bedroom department and I knew it wasn't really feasible to have him as a steady boyfriend again. It would be a step back and I was sure the same old stuff would come up again. Now that we'd been down on land for a few hours, my earlier resolve had returned and I knew that I didn't want things to go back to how they were.

'Oh Tony, you know it doesn't work for all sorts of reasons. You'll be off to university soon —'

'September or even October, that's ages away.'

'Yes but it's not just that. You want more than me —'

'No,' he said. 'I realised when you were away. I'd rather be with you and not have sex than be with someone I'm not that into who will have sex. I can change my university application. I could go to one in London and then we'd be together.'

'No way! You've wanted to go to Oxford since I've known you. It will be fab there, don't even talk about staying in London. I would really really *really* hate that you would do something like that for me.'

'I would. Honest Lucy, I think we should get back together and, OK, so maybe I'll go to Oxford but it's not far. You can come there and I can travel back.'

As I watched him plead with me, it was weird. Here was everything I wanted from Tony, but I knew with complete certainty that we should both be free. Him to enjoy his time being a student. I didn't want him meeting some babe then resenting that he had a girlfriend back in London. And I had only had three boyfriends: Tony, Daniel and Teddy – and Teddy was only a holiday romance. Whatever. I was too young to be tied to one person. *Amazing,* I thought, *because when I first met him, I would have given anything to be his girlfriend for ever, anything – but I feel like I've grown up since then.* I realised that I had changed and, although I still rated Tony totally, I didn't think the time was right for us to get serious. Plus, he always started up eventually with the wandering hands and then I felt torn between wanting to go ahead and feeling pressured.

'Oh I don't know what I want, Tone. Can't we take a break from it all for a while? Just be mates? I do know that I want to be friends whatever happens.' We both smiled when I said that because we both knew that it was that same old line. 'You know I like you loads,' I continued.

Tony smiled sadly. 'Yeah, yeah and *don't* say the "It's not you, it's me" line too or I may have to kill myself.'

I reached out my hand to him and he took it and for a few moments we stayed like that, holding hands and looking into each other's eyes. If I hadn't been feeling unwell, I'd have pulled him in closer.

We let go of each other's hands and he went to the door. 'Later then, Lovering.'

'Later,' I said.

He half opened the door and went out, then he put his head back. 'Still friends though?'

'Always,' I said. 'And I'm always up for movies, coffees . . .'

Tony grinned. 'Bar mitzvahs, weddings and funerals. I may just take you up on a movie sometime, hey?'

'I'll be there.'

And then he left.

Normally I would have called one of the girls, or all of them, to let them know the latest but my stomach gurgled and another wave of sickness came over me – plus I needed some time alone. Although saying no to Tony felt like the best option for the time being, it made me feel sad. I couldn't help thinking of what might have been and, as I snuggled down under my duvet, I remembered all the great times we'd had together and how I felt when I was with him. I wondered if I'd made the right decision after all.

Tony

'So how did it go with the lovely Lucy?' asked Rob as we sat waiting for our biology class to begin. 'Do I hear wedding bells?'

I shook my head. 'Change of plan. Had to let her down gently.'

Rob looked puzzled. 'But I thought you were going to . . . you know . . . declare your love on bended knee.'

'Nah. Changed my mind. I mean, she's a kid and she's really into me. I thought it best to make a clean break. I don't want to mess her around – you know what I'm like and Lucy deserves better.'

Rob grinned. 'Andrea.'

I nodded. 'Andrea.'

'Oxford.'

I nodded again. 'Oxford and a million girls waiting for the love meister.'

So Andrea hadn't told them that I hadn't taken up her

offer down in Brighton? Just like I hadn't told Rob that Lucy hadn't taken up mine. *I guess everyone has their pride,* I thought as Dr Roberts arrived and took his place behind his desk.

Lucy

Lucy's diary

3rd May

Note to self – write your diary more often!

Life has been full-on lately. Ever since I got back from Florence. First of all, Nesta, Izzie and I went to the pilot for a new TV show called *Teen Talk* and Izzie got to sing when the artiste who was supposed to play got delayed on the train. She was so brilliant and got a ton of fan letters afterwards, which was exactly what she needed because she's been through hell in the lurve department recently.

First of all, Jay, the boy she met in Italy, turned out to be a love rat because he had a girlfriend back here that oops, he just forgot to mention. Then she got into a whole self-loathing thing about her shape, which is mad – she thinks she is big and boys won't like her when actually she is just curvy and gorgeous and boys adore her. And then to top it all, she went and fell for a guy she met at the *Teen Talk* show who turned out to be gay. I think they're going to be mates though – like me and Tony, although Tony and I do have the occasional snog still every now and then. Like last night – it was the Diamond Destiny ball and I couldn't resist him, he looked so gorgeous dressed up in black tie, like a prince. The ball was for charity. All Nesta's idea. She went a bit OTT at first and laid an ENORMOUS guilt trip on us all about all the poor and sick in the world – typical Nesta – but in the end, it was a gas and we raised a ton of dosh. What's more, Nesta got off with William Lewis, a boy she met at the history project do. I think love is deffo in the air there. Of all the boys I have ever seen her with, he's the one I'd say is her match, and that's saying something.

I don't want a boyfriend at the moment. I like the way things are with Tony, no pressure because we're not 'in a relationship' but he calls me often and I feel that I can call him anytime. I know that he'd be there for me if I ever needed. I also know that he isn't seeing anyone else at the mo. Nesta keeps me filled in. He's studying like mad because he really wants to get the grades for Oxford.

Feeling good about life lately. I *like* being single. It's liberating! No having to worry about whether he'll phone or if I said the wrong thing or can he be trusted and will he come on too strong and all the stuff. Yay.

Tony

I had booked Biasi's for the day after Lucy's birthday in May. We had been there a few times and now we thought of it as *our* special place. We had our usual table and had our usual meals. Pizza for Lucy and *pasta alla vongole* for me.

'So, Lovering, how does it feel to be the ancient age of fifteen?' I asked.

She shrugged and smiled. 'Same as being fourteen but a day older,' she said.

I laughed. 'Any plans for the next year – like succumbing to me and my wicked ways?'

'Yeah, course. Top of my list. Not. We have some plans for the summer holidays though. TJ's Mum and Dad have bought a holiday cottage down in Cornwall . . .'

'Nesta told me. Sounds fab. She said you're all going down.'

Lucy nodded. 'Yeah, but first my whole family is going for a week and then Izzie, TJ and Nesta are coming down later. I can't wait. What about you? Nesta said something about you doing a bit of travelling?'

'Yeah. Me and Rob. Before we get stuck in to the next round of studying.'

She took my hand. 'Big changes coming for you. Moving on.'

I squeezed her hand. 'Not from you. Never from you.'

She let go of my hand and picked up a fork. 'This is my fairy wand – I mean fairy fork – and I hereby free you, free you to go to uni and meet loads of girls, or boys if that takes your fancy, but I free you.'

'Does that mean you don't like me any more?'

Lucy looked sad. 'Never. I will *always* like you.'

I would miss Lucy. Miss her sitting on the end of my bed reading quietly while I did my studying. Miss her knock on the door and her bringing in a bagel or a cake or a CD or some treat to distract me from my work. I'd miss hanging out in Highgate drinking smoothies, going to movies, sitting in the dark holding hands. I'd miss the way her hair smelled of apples and almond. Not that she was the only girl who had been in my life lately. There had been a few. Val, Beth, Sienna, Nicky with a K and Nicci with two Cs. None of them serious though. They were just girls who I'd got off with at parties, girls I'd met at mates' houses, girls at picnics, but no one that had any impact. I didn't want to get tied down, not yet, not with any of them. There was only Lucy who had really got to me. She was completely in tune with me, like just then, doing her fairy spell and letting me go. If only she knew. Setting me free was the perfect way to keep me enslaved to her.

'Hey Lovering, I have an idea,' I said.

She rolled her eyes.

'No. Nothing naughty. No. You set me free. I set you free too, free to snog all those pukey boys that chase after you. I won't object. I won't get jealous – but how about . . . how about we make a promise that when we get to thirty —'

'You get to thirty or I get to thirty?'

'Um, you, that will give me more time —'

'Time to what?'

'Stop butting in. Hear me out. How about when you get to thirty, if you're not with anyone and I'm not with anyone, how about we get together.'

'Get together?' she asked. 'Like now, for a meal?'

'No. As a couple. You, me. Lucy and Tony.'

She laughed, but she didn't say no, then she smiled. 'Want to know a secret?'

'Maybe.'

'It's about you.'

'Definitely then.'

'Remember back when I first met you? Remember I had been looking for a boy at your school? We called him the Mystery Contestant.'

I nodded. I remembered all right. 'Yeah. A boy at my school. You'd been looking for him.'

'He was you,' she blurted. 'I mean, you are he.'

I tried to feign surprise. 'No way! You're kidding. Me? You serious?'

Lucy nodded. 'I went through *agonies*, especially after Nesta introduced you as her brother. I thought I'd never be able to tell anyone.'

I decided to play along. 'Oh God,' I said. 'And I kissed you and you still didn't say anything.'

'I couldn't,' she said. 'And you asked me to describe the boy I was looking for and there you were, standing right in front of me. It was hysterical. Actually it wasn't. At the time, it was a nightmare.'

We sat smiling at each other for a while, holding hands, remembering back then. I wondered whether to tell her my secret – that I'd overheard her talking with the others and had known all along.

Another day, I decided. *Another time . . . because I know that, although our lives may be taking us in different directions, there will be other times with Lucy. Maybe, just maybe, the right time will come to tell her that I've always known that it was me she was looking for.*

The complete

Mates, Dates

The MATES, DATES series

Other series by Cathy Hopkins

Cinnamon Girl

First impressions count. A few weeks after moving to London, India-Jane has managed to convince boy-of-her-dreams Joe that she is an artistic, nit-infested stalker who takes things to extremes. It's not quite the new life she was looking for.

But a fresh start is never easy – starting a new school in Year 11 without looking like a No-mates Nellie, finding real friends who'll share everything with you, discovering what the people you fancy are really like - it's all just a fraction of the mad whirl that is India-Jane's life.

Cathy Hopkins explores, with her trademark wit and wisdom, deeper issues for teens – but with all the humour and cringe-making situations that fans can't get enough of!

The CINNAMON GIRL series

What would you do if you had to tell the complete **truth** for a day? Would you **dare** enter a national singing competition? Could you cope with what happens when you **kiss** the school heart-throb? Could you **promise** to be faithful, whatever form temptation takes?

Becca, Cat, Lia, Squidge and Mac all enjoy playing the *Truth, Dare, Kiss or Promise* game to liven up their lives – but they can never predict where it's going to lead them!

The TRUTH, DARE, KISS, PROMISE series

www.cathyhopkins.com

Get online for the lowdown on
★ the latest news,
★ books,
★ downloads
★ and fab competitions
from Cathy Hopkins!